Just how rich is Mr. Fowler?

"You're going to have to start walking to school now, like the rest of your friends," Mrs. Pervis said. "It will do you good, though. Put some color in your cheeks."

"I can't walk to school, Mrs. Pervis!" Lila cried. "It's way too far."

"Rubbish!" Mrs. Pervis said with a laugh. "It won't take fifteen minutes."

"But Daddy will get a new chauffeur soon, won't he?" Lila asked anxiously.

Mrs. Pervis gave Lila her get-out-of-the-kitchen look. "Your father has a lot on his mind right now, Lila. I don't want you bothering him over this chauffeur business, understand?"

Lila nodded uneasily. She was beginning to have a very bad feeling about things. First, her credit card had been refused. And now Randall had been fired. Was it possible her father was in some kind of financial trouble?

No, Lila told herself. It was probably all just coincidence. Her father was rich, after all. Really rich. He couldn't just lose all that money overnight.

Could he?

Natalie Gau

**SWEET VALLEY TWINS titles, published by Bantam Books.
Ask your bookseller for titles you have missed**

SWEET VALLEY TWINS SUPER CHILLERS

SWEET VALLEY TWINS SUPER EDITIONS

SWEET VALLEY TWINS

Poor Lila!

Written by
Jamie Suzanne

Created by
FRANCINE PASCAL

BANTAM BOOKS
TORONTO • NEW YORK • LONDON • SYDNEY • AUCKLAND

POOR LILA!
A BANTAM BOOK 0 553 40563 2

Originally published in U.S.A. by Bantam Skylark Books

First publication in Great Britain

PRINTING HISTORY
Bantam edition published 1993

Sweet Valley High and Sweet Valley Twins are registered
trademarks of Francine Pascal.

Conceived by Francine Pascal.

Produced by Daniel Weiss Associates, Inc.,
33 West 17th Street, New York, NY 10011

All rights reserved.

Bantam Books are published by Transworld Publishers Ltd.,
61–63 Uxbridge Road, Ealing, London W5 5SA, in Australia
by Transworld Publishers (Australia) Pty. Ltd., 15–25 Helles
Avenue, Moorebank, NSW 2170, and in New Zealand by
Transworld Publishers (N.Z.) Ltd., 3 William Pickering
Drive, Albany, Auckland.

Printed and bound in Great Britain by
Cox & Wyman Ltd., Reading

Poor Lila!

One

You are cordially invited to the annual
UNICORN FOUNDING FLING
*to celebrate a great moment in history:
the founding of the Unicorn Club*

PLACE: *Lila Fowler's estate*
TIME: *Saturday the seventeenth, 2:00 P.M.*
DRESS: *Formal or Fun*

*Don't miss
the most spectacular party
in the history of Sweet Valley!*

Jessica Wakefield read the purple lettering on her invitation one more time as she ran up the stairs. "Elizabeth!" she called, hurrying into her twin sister's bedroom. "Did you get yours yet?"

Elizabeth was sitting at her desk reading her

social studies book. "Get my what?" she asked, sounding distracted.

"Your invitation," Jessica said impatiently. She spotted the purple envelope lying on Elizabeth's dresser and grabbed it. "Lizzie! You haven't even *opened* it!"

Elizabeth shrugged. "You've already told me about the thing at Lila's, Jess."

"The *thing*?" Jessica echoed. "You're talking about the most important party of the year!" She flopped down on Elizabeth's bed. "You could at least try to act a little more excited. I mean, you're really lucky I'm a member of the Unicorns, so I could make sure you'd be invited."

"Practically everyone in the sixth grade is invited," Elizabeth pointed out. "And the seventh. And the eighth. I wouldn't be surprised to hear that the mayor of Sweet Valley was invited, too!"

"Mayor Lodge is busy that day," Jessica said. "But he sent his apologies."

"You actually invited him?" Elizabeth exclaimed with a laugh, staring at her twin in disbelief. "Why would you think the mayor would want to go to a Unicorn party?"

Jessica sighed. Elizabeth had never really appreciated the importance of the Unicorns, even though they were the prettiest, most popular girls at school. But then, Elizabeth felt differently than Jessica did about a lot of things. Although the twins shared identical looks—long, golden-blond hair, blue-green eyes, and dimples in their left cheeks—their different interests and personalities made it easy to tell them apart.

Elizabeth was the more serious, responsible twin. She loved to write, and she was especially proud of her position as editor of *The Sweet Valley Sixers*, the sixth-grade newspaper. She liked to spend her free time reading or talking with close friends like Amy Sutton and Julie Porter.

Jessica, on the other hand, spent almost all of her free time with the other members of the exclusive Unicorn Club. The Unicorns' favorite activities were going to the mall, having parties, and gossiping about boys, clothes, soap operas, and makeup. Every member tried to wear something purple, the color of royalty, every day. And of course, lately the Unicorns had spent a lot of time helping Lila Fowler plan the Founding Fling.

"I just wish you could get a little more excited about the Fling," Jessica complained. "It's going to be awesome! Lila's father's caterer is going to turn the whole estate into a giant luau. Lila got the idea when she and her father went on that weekend trip to Hawaii. There's going to be tons of food, and a live band, and plenty of purple decorations, of course!"

"Of course," Elizabeth said with a wry grin. "Well, it sounds to me like a great chance for Lila to show off."

"Lila can't help it if her dad happens to be

incredibly rich," Jessica said. "I think it's really generous of him to splurge like this."

"It is," Elizabeth agreed. "But it sounds as if Lila's going overboard."

"That's the whole point, Elizabeth," Jessica said. "Anyway, I've got to get over to the mall. The Unicorns are having an important meeting to shop for new outfits for the Fling."

Elizabeth laughed. "So you guys are even holding your meetings at the mall now? I'm surprised Lila's not having the party there!"

"You may laugh now," Jessica said, shaking her finger at her twin, "but just wait. This is going to be the most spectacular party in the history of Sweet Valley Middle School!"

"It isn't easy being rich," Lila Fowler said with a deep sigh. It was Saturday afternoon, and several of the Unicorns were browsing through the racks at Clothes Encounters, a new shop in the Valley Mall.

Jessica rolled her eyes. "Give me a break, Lila," she said. She pulled a suede skirt off a rack, checked the price tag, and quickly put it back.

"It's true," Lila insisted. "Shopping is easier for regular people. When you can afford everything, it makes it so much harder to *choose*."

"Poor Lila!" Mandy Miller said, pretending to wipe away a tear.

Kimberly Haver reached for a purple cashmere

sweater and gasped when she saw the price tag. "I can't afford anything in here!" she whispered. "Maybe we should try Kendall's. They're having a sale."

"No way." Lila flipped her light-brown hair over her shoulder. "This is the only store in the mall that carries these designer labels. Where else am I going to find anything decent to wear to the Fling?" she laughed. "After all, I already own everything they sell at Valley Fashions!"

"We *all* need something new for the party," Janet Howell said. Janet, an eighth-grader, was the president of the Unicorns and Lila's cousin. "I think we should go to a store where we can *all* shop."

"But *I'm* having the party," Lila replied.

"So what? Kimberly had it last year," Janet pointed out. "And we had it at my house the year before. People are still talking about the hayride we had at my Fling, with a wagon and real hay and everything." She paused, and a dreamy smile came over her face. "I spent the whole ride sitting with Chad Lucas, gazing into his beautiful blue eyes."

"I'm sure it was very nice, Janet," Lila said smugly. "But *my* Fling's going to have a ride that will put your hay ride to shame."

"What kind of ride?" Belinda Layton asked.

Lila smiled. "I'll give you a clue. It's big and purple and full of hot air."

"You're giving piggyback rides to all the guests?" Mandy quipped.

While the Unicorns laughed, Lila shot Mandy a dirty look. "Very funny, Mandy," she snapped. "Just for that, you're going to be the last person who gets to ride in my very own personal hot-air balloon."

A hot-air balloon?" Jessica cried. "Your father bought you a hot-air balloon?" She sighed. "I can't even talk my dad into buying me a new bike."

"Actually, Daddy's renting the balloon," Lila replied. "Or he will be, as soon as I tell him to. He's in New York City on business, but he'll be home Tuesday night." She reached into her purse and pulled out a page torn from a magazine. "See, I noticed this last night in the back of *California Monthly*."

The Unicorns gathered around to see the photograph of a huge purple balloon, soaring high over a ridge of hills. "It's beautiful," Ellen Riteman exclaimed.

"The ad says you can rent it by the day," Lila said. "I'm sure Daddy won't mind getting it for me. Can't you just picture this incredible purple balloon floating over my house? Look, the ad says you can even have a special banner made to hang on the basket."

"Like, 'Come one, Come all, to the Unicorn

Founding Fling,' " Jessica suggested. "People will see it for miles around."

Janet shook her head. "Bad idea, Jess. We don't want just *any*body showing up at our party."

Mandy laughed. "We invited practically the entire town, Janet."

Belinda shook her head. "I can't believe your father's going to rent one of those balloons. It must cost a ton of money."

Lila folded up the picture and put it back in her purse. "Daddy's very generous," she said, picking up the cashmere sweater Kimberly had been admiring. "I guess he spoils me a little because he's away so much on business trips."

"A *little*?" Jessica teased. "That's the understatement of the century!"

"Besides," Lila added, ignoring Jessica, "he understands that it's my duty to entertain my friends. That's just one of the burdens of being rich."

Jessica rolled her eyes. "Why don't we burdens head over to Kendall's?" she suggested.

"Yeah, we regular people can't afford this shop," Mandy added with a grin.

"All right, already," Lila said. "Just let me pick up a couple of odds and ends." She picked up two of the purple cashmere sweaters. "These are much too casual for the party, of course," she said. "But they'll be okay for hanging around the house in."

"But that sweater costs ninety dollars!" Jessica cried. "You call that casual?"

"Why are you getting two?" Ellen asked, sounding hopeful. "By the way, have I ever mentioned that you and I wear exactly the same size?"

"The extra's not for you, Ellen," Lila replied. "It's for me, as a back-up."

"A back-up?" Jessica repeated.

Lila nodded. "In case the other one's at the dry cleaners when I want to wear it." She marched to the counter at the back of the store and put down the two sweaters. "That'll be a charge," she said as she took her wallet out of her purse. She pulled out a shiny gold credit card and handed it to the clerk.

"How many credit cards do you have, anyway?" Ellen asked, peering over Lila's shoulder.

Lila shrugged. "Search me. I lost count a long time ago. Anyway, my purse got so heavy that I had to start leaving most of them at home."

Jessica patted her on the shoulder. "We hate to see you suffering so much, Lila."

"Suffering?" Ellen repeated. "Lila's not suffering! She's the only girl in the sixth grade I know who even *has* credit cards."

"Jessica was being sarcastic, Ellen." Lila explained. "Which is too bad, because I *never* lend my sweaters to sarcastic people—"

"Ms. Fowler?" the clerk interrupted.

"Yes?" Lila said.

"I'm afraid I'm having some trouble with your credit card," the clerk whispered.

"What do you mean, *trouble*?" Lila demanded loudly.

"The computer won't accept it. Perhaps you'd like to try another card."

"I left my other cards at home!" Lila snapped.

"They were weighing her down," Ellen added helpfully.

The clerk cleared her throat. "I'm sure it's just a computer glitch," she said quickly. "I'll try running it through again."

"Stupid store," Lila muttered while the clerk tried the card again. "I'm never coming here again, designer clothes or not."

"Maybe Uncle George forgot to pay his bill," Janet teased.

"Or maybe he's gone broke," Jessica added, as the girls burst into laughter.

The clerk returned, shaking her head. "I'm terribly sorry, Ms. Fowler," she said. "Maybe you'd like to pay cash today instead."

"I don't *have* that much cash with me!" Lila cried. She leaned over the counter and glared at the clerk. "Do you know who I am? Have you ever heard of Fowler Systems International?"

"Um," the clerk began nervously. "Don't they have something to do with computers?"

Lila nodded. "Well, my father *owns* Fowler

Systems," she said. "And he could buy a million of these stupid sweaters if he felt like it!"

"But they're women's sweaters, Lila—" Ellen pointed out.

"Shut up, Ellen!" Lila commanded. "Now, are you going to let me buy these sweaters or not?"

"I—I can't," the clerk stammered.

"Lila," Mandy interjected. "It's not her fault there's a problem with your credit card."

"There's nothing wrong with this card!" Lila shouted. "I've used it a zillion times!"

"I'm really sorry, Ms. Fowler," the clerk said softly.

"Just forget it!" Lila snapped. She stuffed the card into her wallet and stomped toward the door, her giggling friends trailing behind her.

"It's not funny," she said angrily when they were back out in the mall. "This has never, ever happened to me before. It's humiliating."

"Lighten up, Lila," Jessica said. "It's probably just what the clerk said—a computer glitch." She took her friend by the arm. "Come on, let's go get some frozen yogurt."

Lila glanced back at the shop and sighed. "Oh, all right."

"It'll be my treat," Jessica added. She grinned at the other Unicorns. "That is, of course, unless you want to charge it!"

Two

◇

"So, how're the Wingding plans coming?" Steven, the twins' fourteen-year-old brother, asked Monday evening as the family sat down to dinner.

"It's *Fling*, for your information," Jessica retorted as she buttered her baked potato. She turned to Elizabeth. "Today Lila decided to order souvenir T-shirts for all the guests. Can you believe it?"

"Yes, actually I *can* believe it," Elizabeth replied in a bored voice.

"This party sounds as if it's going to cost Lila's father a small fortune," Mr. Wakefield remarked.

"It is," Jessica said proudly. "And the Unicorns are going to be incredibly busy for the next couple of weeks, planning all the important details.

I'll barely have time to keep up with my homework."

"I'm sure you'll manage somehow," Mrs. Wakefield said with a warning look.

"I guess this means you won't be able to do the volunteer work Mrs. Arnette was talking about in social studies today," Elizabeth said, feeling a little disappointed.

"What kind of volunteer work, honey?" Mrs. Wakefield asked as she reached for a roll.

"We're studying the problem of homelessness in Sweet Valley and around the country," Elizabeth explained. "Mrs. Arnette thought it would be nice if our class volunteered at the day-care center at the Sweet Valley Homeless Shelter. Children stay there during the day while their parents are out looking for work."

"What would you be doing there?" Mr. Wakefield asked.

Elizabeth took a sip of her milk. "I'm not exactly sure. Mostly baby-sitting, I guess. But it seems like a good way to help out." She looked over at Jessica, who was concentrating very hard on scooping up peas with her spoon.

"I think it's a great idea," Mrs. Wakefield said. "Who else is volunteering with you?"

"Well, Amy wants to, but she has a huge science project due this week. And Julie has extra flute lessons after school to get ready for her next recital. But Melissa McCormick promised to go with me." Elizabeth glanced at Jessica again. "I was hoping maybe you'd want to come along too, Jess."

Jessica stopped playing with her peas. "Elizabeth, I *hate* it when you do this to me!"

"Do what?" Elizabeth demanded.

"Make me look bad."

"You don't need Elizabeth for that," Steven said with a laugh. "You do a great job all on your own."

"Shut up, Steven, or I'll *un*invite you to Lila's party," Jessica warned.

"Please, no! Anything but that!" Steven cried, pretending to be horrified. "My social life would be ruined—"

"Couldn't you come just one afternoon?" Elizabeth interrupted. "We were planning to go on Wednesday."

"I'd *like* to, I really would," Jessica said. "But I'm just way too busy right now."

"Well, I think you're doing a wonderful thing, Elizabeth," Mrs. Wakefield said.

"I hope so," Elizabeth said doubtfully. "Sometimes I wonder how much difference one person can really make."

"The important thing is that you care enough to try," Mr. Wakefield assured her.

Jessica cleared her throat. "I *also* care about

the, uh . . . the underprivileged. But I can't turn my back on my best friend when she needs my help, can I?"

Elizabeth shrugged. "We understand, Jess. You're volunteering, in your own way. Only you're volunteering to help the *over*privileged!"

That evening, Lila was in her bedroom working on plans for the Fling when she heard loud voices downstairs.

"Mrs. Pervis?" Lila called, stepping into the hallway.

Mrs. Pervis was the Fowlers' housekeeper. Lila's parents had divorced when she was very young, and Mrs. Pervis was almost like a mother to her, especially when Mr. Fowler was away on one of his frequent business trips.

"Is that you, Mrs. Pervis?" Lila called a little louder.

There was no answer. Lila paused at the head of the stairs, listening to the voices below. One of them belonged to Mrs. Pervis, and she sounded angry.

Lila headed down the stairs. The argument seemed to be coming from the kitchen. Slowly she tiptoed across the large marble entryway toward the closed kitchen door.

"Look, there's no point in getting upset with *me*," she heard Mrs. Pervis say forcefully. "I'm just telling you what Mr. Fowler said."

"Why doesn't he tell me himself, instead of getting you to do his dirty work?" someone demanded. Lila recognized the voice. It was Randall, her father's chauffeur.

"You know as well as I do that he's away on business," Mrs. Pervis exclaimed. "I don't like having to do this, but he left me very specific instructions—fire Randall immediately."

Lila gasped. Her father was firing Randall? How would she get to school without a chauffeur?

"Why does he want to fire me?" Randall asked loudly.

"You know very well why," Mrs. Pervis said. "It has to do with the money."

"Like he doesn't have enough?" Randall demanded.

"That's not the point," Mrs. Pervis said. "Let's just say he doesn't have enough for what you seem to need."

Lila's jaw dropped. Had she heard Mrs. Pervis correctly? Was it really possible that Randall was being fired because Mr. Fowler was having money problems?

"I'll take the keys to the cars now," Mrs. Pervis said firmly.

A moment later, Lila heard the jangle of keys as Randall tossed them onto the kitchen table.

"Here! And good riddance to you and Fowler," Randall said angrily. "See how he likes driving himself around."

Suddenly the kitchen door flew open, nearly knocking Lila into the wall. Randall stormed by without even noticing her.

"Mrs. Pervis?" Lila said, rushing into the kitchen.

"Good riddance, himself," Mrs. Pervis muttered. She looked at Lila and shook her head. "I suppose you were listening at the door?"

Lila nodded.

"Well, it had to be done," Mrs. Pervis said. "And I'm glad it's over with."

"I never did like Randall very much, anyway," Lila admitted. "He was always calling me La-la. And he played really awful country songs on the car radio."

"You may miss him when he's gone," Mrs. Pervis warned. "You're going to have to start walking to school now, like the rest of your friends. It will do you good, though. Put some color in your cheeks."

"I can't walk to school, Mrs. Pervis!" Lila cried. "It's way too far!"

"Rubbish," Mrs. Pervis said with a laugh. "It won't take fifteen minutes."

"This is horrible," Lila moaned. "Why did Daddy want you to fire Randall, anyway?"

Mrs. Pervis shook her head. "It's a long story, dear, and I've got a kitchen to clean up."

"But he'll hire a new chauffeur soon, won't he?" Lila asked anxiously.

Mrs. Pervis gave Lila her get-out-of-the-kitchen look. "Your father has a lot on his mind right now, Lila. I don't want you bothering him over this chauffeur business, understand?"

Lila nodded uneasily. She was beginning to have a very bad feeling about things. First her credit card had been refused. Now Randall had been fired. Was it possible that Mr. Fowler was in some kind of financial trouble?

No, Lila told herself. It was probably all just coincidence. Her father was rich, after all. Really rich. He couldn't just lose all that money overnight.

Could he?

The next afternoon, Lila went to the school library when the last bell rang. She stayed there, pretending to work on her homework, until she was certain that all her friends had left. There was no point in humiliating herself by letting them see her walk home, she figured, especially since it was only temporary. Her father was coming home tonight, and despite what Mrs. Pervis had said, Lila was certain that he would hire a new chauffeur right away.

When the coast was clear, she set out for her house. By the time she'd gone a block, her feet began to ache. She was wearing a brand-new pair of very expensive Italian leather flats. The shoes looked great with her outfit, but unfortunately they weren't very comfortable for walking any distance. *This is so unfair*, she told herself as she trudged along. *Rich people aren't supposed to have to walk home from school.*

Suddenly she had a queasy feeling in the pit of her stomach. What if she really wasn't rich anymore? She'd asked herself that question a thousand times that day. And no matter how hard she tried to tell herself it was crazy to worry, the question wouldn't go away.

By the time Lila neared home, she was certain she had blisters on every one of her toes. As she turned the corner and glanced down the street, she was surprised to see a cab pulling into the Fowlers' long driveway.

"Daddy!" she cried when she saw her father emerge from the backseat. Forgetting her aching feet, she ran the rest of the way home and dashed through the front door.

Mr. Fowler was in the entryway, setting down his briefcase. "How's my girl?" he asked as Lila ran to give him a hug.

"I missed you so much!" Lila exclaimed. Seeing her father standing there in his crisp gray business suit made her feel much better. All her worries about money suddenly seemed silly.

"Did you bring me anything?" Lila asked eagerly.

"Sorry, honey. Not this time. I had a rough week in New York, and there just wasn't time."

Lila's smile faded. Her father practically always brought her presents back from his trips. Still, she reminded herself, he'd said he was too busy. It wasn't as though he couldn't *afford* to get her something.

Mr. Fowler removed his overcoat and handed it to Mrs. Pervis. "Everything go OK?" he asked.

"Just fine, sir," Mrs. Pervis said. "I took care of Randall, like you said."

Mr. Fowler frowned. "At least we got rid of him before he cost us too much more."

Lila swallowed past a lump in her throat. *Before he cost us too much more?* Did her father mean they couldn't afford a chauffeur any longer?

"Daddy?" Lila said quietly. "When are you going to hire a new chauffeur?"

"What, honey?" Mr. Fowler asked distractedly as he thumbed through a pile of mail on the table in the entryway.

"When are we getting someone to replace Randall?"

Mr. Fowler rubbed his brow. "We'll see how things go," he answered vaguely. "I've got a lot on my mind right now, Lila." He opened a long white envelope and began reading the letter inside.

Lila nervously pushed her hair behind her ears. At least her father hadn't said no. She hesitated for a moment. "Daddy?"

"Hmm?"

"I've got something important to ask you."

Mr. Fowler didn't look up. "Ask away."

Good, Lila thought. Her father was preoccupied. He always said *yes* when he was thinking about something else.

"Can I have a purple hot-air balloon at my Founding Fling?"

Mrs. Pervis chuckled as she walked away, shaking her head.

"Balloons?" Mr. Fowler said absentmindedly. "Sure thing. Have all the balloons you want."

"I just need one."

"One balloon?" Mr. Fowler looked up from his letter.

"It's a hot-air balloon. You know—the kind with a basket that takes people up in the air. I saw an advertisement for a place where you can rent them by the day."

"Why on earth do you need a hot-air balloon at this party?" Mr. Fowler asked irritably. "I've spent hours arranging for the caterer and the decorator and the music, and now you want a hot-air balloon?"

"But—" Lila began. She paused and let her lower lip tremble just a little. Tears never failed to change her father's mind. "But it's a *purple* balloon, Daddy!"

"No," Mr. Fowler said firmly. "It's out of the question, Lila. I just can't manage it right now."

Lila couldn't believe her ears. "But I've already promised everyone!" she protested.

"Well, I guess you'll just have to *un*promise them," Mr. Fowler said as he scanned another letter.

Lila sniffled loudly.

Her father looked up and smiled sympathetically. "I'm sorry, honey," he said. "But we all have to make sacrifices sometimes."

Lila watched forlornly as her father disappeared into his study. *Make sacrifices?* she thought. Rich people didn't make sacrifices!

That is, unless they weren't rich anymore.

Three

"I guess we're the only ones who showed up," Elizabeth said glumly on Wednesday afternoon. She and Melissa stood outside the Sweet Valley Homeless Shelter's day-care center. The center was a simple, single-story building that was decorated with a mural of happy children playing in a brightly colored garden.

"To tell you the truth, I'm not really surprised," Melissa replied. "A lot of kids are glad to volunteer if you want them to help with something like the Unicorns' skate-a-thon, or that bike-a-thon the PTA had a while ago. But they think doing this kind of volunteer work is depressing."

Elizabeth glanced at the center's bright yellow front door. "Well, I guess we should head inside," she said hesitantly.

"Are you nervous?" Melissa asked.

"A little," Elizabeth admitted. "I've never really done anything like this before."

"I'm sure they'll be glad to have us help out," Melissa said.

Elizabeth hoped Melissa was right. She really had been looking forward to helping at the center, but now that she and Melissa were actually here, she was beginning to have some second thoughts. It was hard to imagine how two sixth-graders could help with a problem as enormous as homelessness. Still, she wanted to try.

"Who have we here?" a woman's voice demanded.

Elizabeth and Melissa both spun around. Standing behind them was a pretty young woman with dark, curly hair. "I'm Elizabeth Wakefield," Elizabeth said. "And this is Melissa McCormick. We're the volunteers from Mrs. Arnette's class at Sweet Valley Middle School."

"Volunteers, huh?" the woman said. She was smiling, but she sounded skeptical. "Well, we'll see how long you last." She looked them over carefully. "So come on in. You're not doing any good standing around out on the sidewalk."

Melissa gave Elizabeth a nervous glance as they followed the woman into the day-care center.

"My name is Connie," the woman said over her shoulder as she led them through a room filled with small tables and chairs. "This is a day-care center run for the children of homeless people. Most of the people who live at the shelter are out looking for jobs all day long, and they need someone to take care of their kids while they're gone."

"We've both baby-sat before," Melissa said.

"That's good," Connie said. "These kids can be a handful."

Elizabeth and Melissa followed her into another room, a little larger than the first. About a dozen children were there, running around or playing with the toys that were scattered around everywhere. Two adults were trying to keep up with the kids, but it was obvious that they could use some help. A baby was howling, two little girls were arguing loudly over a doll, and in the corner, a red-haired boy was writing his name on the wall with a marking pen.

"You forgot the 'H' again, John," Connie called to the boy. "And next time try using a piece of paper, OK, kiddo?"

"What should we do first?" Elizabeth asked, looking around at the chaotic scene.

Connie smiled and pointed at the two little girls, who were still fighting. "You can start by playing referee," she suggested.

Elizabeth and Melissa headed over to the little girls, who were tugging on the arms of a worn-out-looking cloth doll.

"What are your names?" Elizabeth asked.

"Sara," the first girl said, twirling a strand of her silky blond hair around her finger.

The second girl stared at the floor, her face frozen in a pout. "My name's Elizabeth," Elizabeth said, kneeling down and smiling at her. "This is my friend Melissa. Will you tell us your name so we can all be friends?"

"Janie," the second girl answered reluctantly. She reached up and pulled on Melissa's waist-length auburn ponytail. "I want my doll."

"Whose doll is it?" Melissa asked.

"It's *mine*," both girls said in unison.

"Well, I think the answer here is to remember the magic word," Elizabeth said.

"Please?" Sara offered.

"Well, that's *one* magic word," Elizabeth conceded. "But another magic word is *share*. If you two share the doll, you can have a lot more fun."

"Why don't you pretend you're both the baby's big sisters?" Melissa suggested.

"OK," Sara said. "But I'm the *bigger* sister."

"I have a twin sister," Elizabeth said quickly. "Why don't you pretend to be twins? Then you can be exactly the same."

"Are you and your sister exactly the same?" Janie asked.

Elizabeth looked at Melissa and smiled. "Well, maybe not *exactly*," she admitted. "But almost."

"We're twins," Sara exclaimed. "And this is our baby."

Janie nodded, and the two little girls walked off contentedly, each holding the doll by one arm.

Connie had been watching. "You handled that well," she remarked. "They won't all be that easy, though."

"We know," Melissa said. "But don't worry, we won't give up."

"Like I said, we'll see," Connie said. "How are you two at making peanut-butter-and-jelly sandwiches?"

"Actually, they're my specialty," Elizabeth replied.

"Good. We always feed the kids a snack in the late afternoon," Connie said. "Usually peanut butter and jelly and a glass of juice."

She led Elizabeth and Melissa to a tiny kitchen off the main room. "We have thirteen kids here today, not counting the babies, plus our adult volunteers and you two." Connie counted on her fingers as she spoke. "Go ahead and make about twenty sandwiches. That way the kids who are big eaters can have an extra."

Suddenly the sound of angry cries drifted in from the main room.

"So much for the truce you arranged between Sara and Janie," Connie said with a laugh. "I'll go try my hand at it while you two start on the food."

It took about half an hour for the girls to

assemble the sandwiches and pile them on a serving tray. When Elizabeth carried the tray into the
main room, all the children crowded around, except for one little boy who hung back behind the
others. He had long, light-brown hair and huge
blue eyes. Elizabeth watched him for a while,
wondering if she should encourage him to eat.

After a few minutes, Elizabeth went to a
changing table to help Melissa diaper one of the
babies. When she glanced back, she happened to
see the little boy quickly pick up one of the sandwiches and hide it in the large pocket of his jacket.
Then he picked up a second sandwich and began
to eat it.

"Did you see that?" Elizabeth whispered.

"See what?" Melissa asked.

"That little boy. He hid a sandwich in his jacket.
Doesn't he know he can have a second sandwich if
he wants one? He doesn't have to sneak."

"Maybe it's some kind of game," Melissa suggested. "You know how little kids are."

Elizabeth shrugged. "Maybe." She and Melissa watched as the boy sidled toward the door
leading out to the playground behind the building.
With a last glance around, he disappeared outside.

"Who's that little boy?" Elizabeth asked when
Connie passed by. "The one with the pretty blue
eyes?"

"Blue eyes," Connie said, tapping her finger
on her chin. "Oh, you must mean David Lowell."

"David," Elizabeth repeated thoughtfully.

"Is anything wrong?"

"No," Elizabeth said hastily, glancing toward the door. She didn't want to get the little boy in trouble, but she decided to keep an eye on him herself—just in case.

"Uh-oh," Jessica said as she stood in the hot lunch line on Thursday. "I forgot my wallet again."

She turned to Lila, who was standing behind her. "Could you just put it on your credit card for me, Lila?"

"Very funny, Jessica," Lila snapped. She'd been listening to the Unicorns' credit card jokes all week, and she was getting awfully tired of them. Usually she loved it when her friends teased her about being rich, but she was in no mood for their jokes about money now that she was worried she might not have any anymore.

"How many times do I have to tell you?" Lila muttered as she and Jessica sat down at the Unicorns' table, which they called the Unicorner. "My father said that the credit-card mess was just a computer foul-up. He's already taken care of it."

The truth was, she hadn't exactly asked her father about the reason her credit card had been refused. She'd planned to, but he'd seemed so preoccupied the past few days that she hadn't wanted to bother him. Also, she was afraid of what his answer might be.

"Sure, Lila," Jessica said. "Whatever you say."

"It's true!" Lila cried. "If I wanted to, I could go back to Clothes Encounters right now and buy each of you ten sweaters."

"Sure, Lila," Janet said.

"Sure, Lila," Ellen repeated, shaking her head.

"Why won't anyone believe me?" Lila demanded.

"We're just giving you a hard time, Lila," Jessica replied. "Don't be so sensitive." She looked around the table, smiling. "In fact, to prove that I believe you, I'm going to let you charge me a new bike."

"I could use some jewelry," Tamara Chase added as she opened a carton of milk. "Gold would be nice."

"No, diamonds," Mandy corrected. "Definitely diamonds. They're a girl's best friend, you know." She grinned. "That is, if you can afford them."

"Lila can afford them," Jessica exclaimed. "She'll just *charge* them!"

Lila started to form a retort, but just then Elizabeth and Melissa walked by the Unicorner, carrying a large carton.

"What's in the box?" Jessica called out.

"Nothing, yet," Elizabeth replied, walking over. "It's for clothing donations for the homeless shelter."

"I've got a ton of clothes I could donate," Lila said quickly, feeling grateful for the chance to change the subject.

"Great," Melissa said. "Bring them to school this week, and we'll take them over to the shelter."

"Can't someone from the shelter come by my house to pick the stuff up?" Lila asked. "I don't want to have to carry it all that way, especially now that my chauffeur's—" she hesitated, "sick."

"What's wrong with Randall?" Jessica asked.

Lila stared at her plate of meat loaf. She hadn't meant to let anyone know that she was walking to school these days. Whatever she came up with to explain Randall's absence, it had better sound serious and *very* long-lasting. She took a deep breath. "Randall has, uh, beriberi."

"Beri-what?" Jessica asked. She didn't sound entirely convinced.

"Beriberi," Lila repeated.

"Is it serious?" Ellen asked.

"Very," Lila said. "He may not be back for months. In the meantime, I'm going to walk to school."

"Lila Fowler, walk to school? I don't believe my ears!" Jessica exclaimed.

"I wondered why you were rubbing your feet during homeroom," Ellen added.

"I don't mind walking," Lila replied. "It's the least I can do until Randall recovers. You know how close we were."

"You hate Randall," Jessica said, narrowing her eyes suspiciously. "He's the one who's always calling you La-la."

Melissa cleared her throat. "Well, maybe I could stop by your house and pick up your clothes for the shelter, Lila. I mean, since your chauffeur is sick and all. Would that be OK?"

"Sure," Lila said. As she watched Melissa and Elizabeth walk off, she sighed with relief. The last thing she felt like doing was trudging to school carrying a bunch of her old clothes.

"You know," she whispered when Melissa was out of earshot, "Melissa ought to think about accepting some clothing donations herself. Her outfits are always about two years out of date."

"Just because her family isn't rich doesn't give you the right to be so critical," Mandy snapped.

"I wasn't trying to be critical," Lila said, feeling a little guilty. She hadn't meant to be mean. She was just trying to sound like her usual rich self, even if she wasn't feeling like it. "I was just giving out a little free fashion advice."

"Well, try to be a little more sensitive," Mandy said. "Not everyone has as much money as you do, Lila."

"*No one* has as much money as I do," Lila replied automatically, but as soon as the words were out of her mouth, she felt that queasy feeling in the pit of her stomach again.

"Speaking of money, Lila," Janet said. "What did Uncle George say about the hot-air balloon?"

Great, Lila thought angrily. *Here comes another lie.* Usually she didn't mind lying—in fact, she was a real pro. But this whole conversation was making her increasingly uncomfortable.

"Daddy thought it was a great idea," Lila answered at last.

"Big surprise," Janet said. "Has he ever said no to anything you wanted?"

"Once," Ellen reminded her. "Remember when you wanted him to hire a full-time tutor to do your homework for you, Lila?"

"That's the only time he said no," Lila said uneasily. "And anyway, he absolutely *loved* the idea of a balloon."

"This is so exciting," Kimberly exclaimed. "Now your only problem is deciding what to put on the balloon banner."

I wish that were my only problem, Lila thought grimly. How much longer could she go on telling lies and pretending everything was all right?

She knew she was going to have to talk to her father—tonight. She vowed to herself to ask him straight out if they were poor.

She tried not to think about what she'd do if his answer was yes.

Four

◇

"Daddy?" Lila called out softly that afternoon. She had been standing in front of the big oak door to his study for the last five minutes, trying to decide whether she should knock.

"I'm on the phone, honey," Mr. Fowler called back. "Can it wait?"

"Sure," Lila answered. She slumped against the wall and sighed. Sure, it could wait. She was really in no hurry to find out that she'd gone overnight from being rich and happy to being poor and miserable.

Just then the doorbell chimed. "I'll get it, Mrs. Pervis," Lila called. She swung open the door and was surprised to see Melissa standing there, holding a large, empty cardboard box.

"Hi, Lila," Melissa said. "I hope you don't mind my coming over unannounced like this, but

I was just passing by so I thought I'd stop in and see if I could pick up those clothes now."

"Clothes?" Lila repeated blankly.

"You know. For the shelter," Melissa said. "Remember, today at lunch you said—"

"Oh, *those* clothes," Lila said. "To tell you the truth, I really don't feel like—"

"I'll help you sort through your stuff if you want," Melissa interrupted. "I don't mean to be pushy, but there's really an urgent need for clothes down at the shelter."

Just then a sharp noise, like a gun shot, echoed down the street.

"Duck!" Lila cried with a start.

"Sorry," Melissa said, her cheeks coloring just a little. "That was our old Dodge." She pointed across the Fowler's wide, manicured lawn to an ancient blue car that was parked by the curb, belching smoke. "I think it just backfired," she explained. "It sort of has chronic indigestion."

"You call that a car?" Lila said, staring at the funny-looking old heap.

"Hey, it's got four wheels and it runs," Melissa said with a shrug. "In my book, that's a car."

"In *my* book, that's a junk heap," Lila responded. "Do you think maybe you could park a little farther down the street? I wouldn't want people to think it belongs to us."

Melissa pursed her lips. "I guess I could ask Andy to move it—"

"Andy? Your brother?" Lila asked, suddenly very interested. She'd met Melissa's brother once at a party at Jessica's house. He was very tall, very nice, and *very* cute. Unfortunately, he was also very old, an actual senior in high school. *But*, Lila thought, *I am very mature for my age.* "That's OK, don't bother," she told Melissa quickly. "What's a little rust among friends?" She stepped back so Melissa could enter. "Come on in. I'll help you load up that box, and I'll even help you carry it down to the car."

"This is really nice of you, Lila," Melissa said as she stepped into the entryway.

"No biggie," Lila said with a wave of her hand. "I've been meaning to clean out my closets, anyway. And after all, it is for a worthy cause." *And I'll get to say hi to Andy as a reward for my good deed*, she added to herself.

Halfway up the curving staircase, Lila paused and looked back. Melissa was still standing in the entryway, staring at the huge, glittering chandelier overhead. "You coming, Melissa?" Lila asked.

"Oh, sorry," Melissa said. She reached for her box and ran up the stairs. "It's just that I've never seen such an amazing house. It looks like something out of a movie."

"I thought you'd been here before," Lila said when they reached the top of the stairs. "Didn't you come to my party last month?"

"You didn't invite me," Melissa reminded her with a smile.

"Oh," Lila said uncomfortably. She'd forgotten. The truth was, she and Melissa traveled in different circles. Melissa hung around with people like Elizabeth Wakefield and Amy Sutton. *Boring* people.

"You got an invitation to the Unicorn Founding Fling, didn't you?" Lila asked.

"Everyone did," Melissa replied with a laugh.

"It's going to be a spectacular party," Lila said as the girls headed into her bedroom.

"So I hear." Melissa set down the box. "Nice bedroom."

"You think so?" Lila asked. "I'm thinking about having it redecorated." *That is, if Daddy still has any money left,* she added to herself. "You know how it is. You get tired of the same old thing." She opened the doors to her huge walk-in closet. "It's actually a good thing you showed up. I've got a ton of old clothes to get rid of."

"Well, I'm sure we can find a good home for whatever you come up with," Melissa said as she sat down on the edge of Lila's bed. "I would never have guessed how much need there is for simple things like clothes and toys at the shelter. Things most of us take for granted."

Lila emerged from the closet carrying an armful of clothes. She held up a green silk dress. "Daddy brought me this from Paris," she said.

"I've never even worn it. It's a designer original, too."

"It's gorgeous," Melissa said.

"Green's not really my color," Lila said with a shrug. "I prefer purple."

She returned to her closet and began to gather up another pile of clothes, but as she did, she felt a sudden unfamiliar wave of panic. Here she was, acting like she always did, as though she could afford to be giving away expensive clothes. What if her father really was broke? Well, even if he was, she decided, she had to keep up appearances.

She stepped out of the closet. Melissa was standing in front of Lila's full-length mirror, holding the green dress in front of her. "Oh, hi," she said, turning around. She folded the dress and laid it in the box.

"Why don't you keep that dress, Melissa?" Lila suggested. "It'd look great with your eyes."

"I couldn't," Melissa said. "There are a lot of people who need it more than I do."

"But you're—" Lila began. *You're poor*, was what she'd almost said. She smiled sheepishly at Melissa, who was shaking her head.

"Lila," Melissa said, "is your mouth actually attached to your brain, or does it just work on auto-pilot?"

"I was only going to say—"

"I *know* what you were going to say," Melissa

said. "And I'll try to believe that your heart was in the right place, as hard as that is."

Lila smiled uncomfortably and gestured toward her dresser. "How about some sweaters?"

"That'd be great," Melissa said. She walked over to join Lila and her eyes fell on a gold framed photograph on the bureau. "Is that—"

"—my mom," Lila finished for her. "She and my dad got divorced when I was little."

Melissa nodded. "Tough, huh?"

Lila knew that Melissa's mother had died recently of a heart attack. "Yeah," she said as her eyes met Melissa's. "I miss her all the time, you know?"

"I know," Melissa said quietly.

Lila handed her a red cardigan sweater. "Melissa," she began, "I don't mean anything when I said—um, started to say—that you were poor."

"I know," Melissa said. "And it's true. We are. But we're lucky compared to a lot of families."

Lila dropped another sweater in the box. "Lucky?"

"Sure. I mean, I have my dad and Andy, and we're really happy."

"Oh." *Of course*, Lila thought to herself, *that's easy for her to say*. Melissa had never been rich, so she didn't have any idea what she was missing. "Well, you're sure you won't take the green dress?"

"Positive," Melissa said. "But not because I'm too proud or anything. The truth is, it *is* a putrid shade of green. No offense."

Lila couldn't help laughing. "Don't tell my dad," she warned. "He's color-blind." She snapped her fingers. "Hey, maybe he has some stuff he could donate. You know, men's clothes."

"That'd be great."

Lila reached for another sweater. "As soon as we're finished here, we'll go ask him. I'm sure he'll be glad to help. Daddy's very generous." *At least he used to be*, she added to herself.

When Lila and Melissa reached Mr. Fowler's study, the door was closed. Lila knocked, then waited for him to answer. He didn't respond, but the girls could hear him talking loudly on the telephone.

"Maybe we should ask him another time," Melissa suggested. "He sounds sort of mad, Lila."

"He always sounds like that," Lila explained. "That's just his business voice."

Melissa examined a portrait hanging in the hallway. "Who's this?" she asked.

"My great-grandma Fowler," Lila said. She laughed. "She's ninety-two and thinks she's Queen Elizabeth most of the time."

"Must run in the family," Melissa said, shaking her head.

"What do you mean?"

Melissa smiled. "You know—thinking you're royalty."

Lila wasn't sure how to respond for a second.

Still, she had the feeling Melissa was laughing with her rather than at her, so she managed a smile.

She knocked again, and when her father didn't answer, she opened the office door a crack. Mr. Fowler was sitting in his brown leather chair with his back to the door.

"Listen, Jim," he said angrily. "I don't know what else to say. This whole set-up is ruined!"

Ruined? Lila felt her stomach do a flip-flop. She glanced back at Melissa, who was still staring up at Great-grandma Fowler.

Lila peeked into her father's study again. He was nodding slowly, while the person on the other end of the phone talked. Suddenly Mr. Fowler slammed his fist down on his desk. "That's not the point!" he yelled. "I'm going to lose a fortune on this deal!"

Lila gasped and quickly shut the door behind her. So it was true. She really was poor. Had Melissa heard? She was still studying the painting intently, but maybe she was just pretending not to have heard so Lila wouldn't be embarrassed. Besides, what could Melissa say? *Sorry to hear you're poor now, Lila. Welcome to the club.* "Daddy's, uh, busy with a big deal right now, Melissa," Lila said quickly.

"That's OK," Melissa said, turning around and looking at Lila. "Lila? Are you OK? You look a little pale."

Lila placed her hand on her forehead. "I think I might be coming down with Randall's beriberi," she said. "It's highly contagious. You probably should be going."

"I'll just go upstairs and get the box," Melissa said.

"Can you do it by yourself?" Lila asked. "I'm going to go get an aspirin."

While Melissa went back upstairs to retrieve the box of clothes, Lila fell into a chair in the hallway and buried her head in her hands. *Ruined*, her father had said. They'd lost a fortune. They were broke. Destitute. Poor.

Good-bye, designer clothes. Good-bye, limousines. Good-bye, happiness and feeling special.

"I hope you feel better, Lila," Melissa said as she returned downstairs, lugging the box.

Lila stood and held open the front door. "Me, too."

"It's probably not beriberi," Melissa advised. "I think that's a pretty rare disease. Maybe you've just got the twenty-four-hour flu."

"I wish it were only going to last twenty-four hours," Lila murmured. "But I'm afraid it may be permanent."

"What?"

"Nothing. See you later, Melissa."

Five

"You're back!" Connie exclaimed on Monday afternoon when Elizabeth and Melissa returned to the day-care center.

"We said we would be," Melissa reminded her.

"Lots of people say that, but once is enough for most of them."

"Look at this box of clothes we brought," Melissa said proudly. She'd spent most of Sunday evening washing and ironing all the donated clothes.

Connie's face broke into a grin. "Not bad," she said. "You two work fast."

"Well, most of it came from one person," Elizabeth admitted.

"She's very rich," Melissa added. "Half these things are designer originals."

"As long as they're warm and comfortable, that's all we care about," Connie said as she lifted the box.

"Did any of the other kids from school show up?" Elizabeth asked.

"Not yet," Connie replied.

"Maybe it'll just take them a while to get up the nerve," Melissa said.

"Well, there's plenty of work to go around if they ever make it. And speaking of work, why don't you get started on the snacks, OK?"

Before they could answer, Connie hustled off toward the office.

"She sure works hard," Melissa observed.

"Everybody here does," Elizabeth said as she and Melissa headed for the kitchen. She looked at Melissa thoughtfully. "Do you really think we're making a difference here, Melissa? I mean, these kids are *homeless*. Compared to their problems, it feels like what we're doing is kind of unimportant." She sighed. "Making them a few peanut-butter sandwiches isn't exactly going to transform their lives."

Melissa paused for a moment. She'd wondered the same thing herself after their first visit to the day-care center. But she'd been thinking about what they'd done that day, and she felt good about it.

"You know," she said at last, "after my mom died, Andy and I went through a really tough time. We were scared and alone and running out of money."

Elizabeth nodded. "I remember."

"Anyway, I've been thinking that when you're feeling like that, little things can be important. I remember how you called to check on me, even though we didn't really know each other that well then. It meant a lot to me." She gazed at the children playing in the main room of the center. "Well, it may not seem like much to us, but I think just coming here and showing these kids we care may make a difference."

The girls went into the kitchen and began making sandwiches. When Elizabeth carried out the loaded tray a few minutes later, the children stopped playing and rushed over, yelling happily. Melissa brought the juice and poured it into paper cups.

"Look," she said, nudging Elizabeth. She nodded toward the corner. "It's that little boy you pointed out before. The one who kind of hangs back behind everyone else."

"Maybe he's just polite."

"No, if that were it, he'd come over now. Everyone else has a sandwich."

"He could be shy."

"Come on," Melissa said. "Let's move away and pretend we're not watching. I want to see if he does the same thing he did last time."

Elizabeth and Melissa wandered away from the table, casually glancing over their shoulders every so often.

"There he goes," Elizabeth said as David sidled over to the sandwiches. "Look."

The little boy picked up one sandwich and quickly slid it into his jacket pocket. Then he picked up a second and began to eat it.

"Just like before," Elizabeth said. "Do you think we should mention it to Connie?"

Melissa shook her head. "Maybe David's been poor so long that he's worried he'll never get enough food again. I know there were times when my family was so broke that I used to feel that way." She paused. "What we need to do is make sure he understands that he can have all the food he wants here."

"There he goes," Elizabeth said. "He's trying to sneak out to the playground again."

"Come on," Melissa urged.

They reached David just as he was backing out the door.

"Hi," Elizabeth said, leaning casually against the door. "Are you David? My name's Elizabeth, and this is Melissa."

The little boy smiled uncertainly. "Yeah. I'm David."

"Did you enjoy the snack?" Melissa asked gently.

"We're just asking because we're the ones who made the sandwiches, and we want to make sure they're good," Elizabeth added.

David nodded thoughtfully. "I guess the sandwich I had was pretty good. It could have used a little less jelly, though. That way it doesn't get soggy."

Melissa grinned. "Next time we'll make one just for you with a little less jelly. But would one be enough?"

David shot her a suspicious glance. "All I can eat is one," he said quickly.

"Well, if you ever want more than that, it's perfectly OK," Melissa assured him. "You could even have three or four if you wanted. Honest."

"One's enough," David said firmly.

Melissa looked at Elizabeth and shrugged helplessly as they watched David walk away.

That afternoon, Lila stayed after school for an hour and a half to practice with the Boosters, the school's baton and cheering squad. The Unicorns had started the Boosters, and all of the members of the squad were Unicorns except for Amy Sutton and Winston Egbert. Usually Lila loved cheering with the Boosters, but today her heart just wasn't in it, and she was half a beat behind on almost every cheer. By the time practice was over, the sky was filled with dark gray clouds. It looked as if it was going to start raining any minute.

Lila walked home as fast as she could, but she was only halfway there when the first heavy drops of rain splattered on her head. Seconds later it began pouring, and Lila was soon drenched to the bone.

She glanced down at her shoes and moaned. They were black suede slip-ons with little bows. Her father had bought them for her in Paris, and she was sure they'd cost him a small fortune. Now the bows were soggy, the suede was muddy, and the shoes were ruined.

So what if my shoes are ruined? Lila thought miserably as she slogged along. *After all, my whole life is ruined.*

She trudged along slowly, ignoring the downpour. Maybe she'd get lucky and catch some horrible disease and die. Beriberi, even. Then at least she wouldn't have to endure this kind of humiliation any longer.

Suddenly Lila jumped as a car backfired loudly behind her.

"Lila?" a voice called out a second later. "Is that you?"

Lila turned to see Melissa leaning her head out of the front window of her old blue car. Andy was driving.

"Come on," Melissa called. "We'll give you a ride home."

Andy slowed the car to a stop and rolled down his window. "Hop in," he urged with a smile.

Lila returned Andy's smile and hesitated. He *was* awfully cute, even driving that hideous car. And he didn't even seem to notice that her hair was hanging in soggy clumps or that her legs were splattered with mud. The inside of the homely old car looked dry and inviting—though of course it couldn't compare to her father's limo.

"OK," she said at last. She splashed over and climbed into the backseat. The upholstery was ripped and stained, and there was a huge pile of newspapers on the other side of the seat.

"Sorry about all the papers," Melissa said. "I do a newspaper route in the mornings, and those are the leftovers. Andy drove me this morning because of the rain."

"You deliver newspapers?" Lila asked doubtfully as she tried to wring out her hair.

"It's a great way to make some extra money," Melissa said. She held up her right arm and flexed her muscle. "Plus, it's great exercise."

Lila tried to imagine delivering papers to help her father out with his money problems. No, she decided, she wasn't the papergirl type. "If I ever got a job," she said, "it would have to be less, um, physical. You know—like being a fashion model, or anchoring the evening news."

Andy and Melissa both laughed, and Lila felt a little hurt. She hadn't been trying to be funny.

"Where to?" Andy asked.

"Lila lives in that mansion up there on the

hill," Melissa said, pointing. "You know, where I picked up those clothes last week." She turned to look at Lila. "How are you feeling, anyway? You shouldn't be walking around in the rain like this, especially since you weren't feeling well last week."

"I'm OK," Lila said with a sigh.

"Lila's chauffeur has beriberi," Melissa told Andy.

Andy grinned. "Sorry to hear it."

"We just dropped Elizabeth off at her house a minute ago," Melissa told Lila. "She and I were over at the shelter. They were really excited about getting those clothes you donated."

"That's nice," Lila said, staring out the window. She was glad it was raining so hard—none of her friends were likely to see her riding around in this old heap.

"I told them your dad might have some stuff to add," Melissa continued.

Not anymore, Lila thought. *We can't afford to give away clothes now.* "I'd ask him, but he's away on business again," she told Melissa.

"When will he get back?" Melissa asked.

"Tomorrow night, I think."

"So who will you have dinner with tonight?"

"The TV," Lila answered. "Usually our housekeeper, Mrs. Pervis, is there. But today is her son's birthday, so she won't be back to our house until late this evening."

"But you can't go home to an empty house," Melissa cried as Andy pulled the car to a stop in front of Lila's drive.

"Sure I can," Lila said wearily, gathering up her backpack. "Mrs. Pervis left my dinner in the refrigerator. All I have to do is put it in the microwave." She frowned. "That is, if I can remember how to work the microwave. She showed me once. How long does it take to heat beef stew? Like an hour?"

"Forget the microwave!" Melissa exclaimed. "You're having dinner with us tonight, Lila."

"Come on," Andy urged. "My dad's an amazing cook."

"I really don't—"

"We won't take no for an answer," Melissa insisted. "It's awful, eating all by yourself."

"Oh, all right," Lila said as she slumped back in her seat. She was too tired to argue. And too depressed to care.

What did it matter where she ate? Her life was over.

Six

◇

"We're having company for dinner, Dad," Melissa called as she led Lila into the McCormicks' kitchen. "Remember Lila Fowler? You met her at the Wakefields' pool party."

Mr. McCormick looked up and smiled broadly. He was tall and thin and looked like an older version of Andy. He was wearing a red apron over faded jeans. "Welcome, Lila," he said as he stirred a large steaming pot on the stove. "Do you like fried eel?"

Lila wrinkled her nose doubtfully. "Well . . . no."

"Good thing we're having spaghetti, then," Mr. McCormick said with a laugh. "Andy, would you make the garlic bread? And Lissa, why don't you and Lila throw together a salad? There are some odds and ends in the fridge, I think."

"Sure, Dad," Melissa said. "But first I'm going to find Lila some dry clothes to wear. She's soaked."

"There's a lot of beriberi going around, you know," Andy added, smiling at Mr. McCormick.

"We'll be right back," Melissa said. "Right after I give Lila the grand tour."

"That should take about ten seconds," Mr. McCormick joked.

Melissa led Lila through a small living room, furnished with old, mismatched furniture and brightly colored pillows. "It's . . . nice," Lila lied, thinking fondly of her own huge living room with its white leather furniture.

"This is my bedroom," Melissa said as she took Lila into a tiny room not much bigger than Lila's walk-in closet at home. "I'll see if I can dig up some clothes for you to wear till yours dry."

"Don't bother, really," Lila said quickly, glancing at Melissa's plain sweater and skirt.

Melissa rolled her eyes. "It won't kill you to wear something for an hour that's not a designer original, Lila."

"Whatever you've got will be fine," Lila said, trying her best to sound gracious. She peered over Melissa's shoulder as she thumbed through the small selection of clothes in her tiny closet. "I prefer natural fabrics," Lila added. "You know . . . linen, silk—"

"Guess you'll just have to rough it." Melissa

tossed her a faded flannel shirt and a pair of old jeans.

"Thanks," Lila said half-heartedly. *I might as well get used to wearing second-hand clothes,* she added to herself.

"I'll go start the salad while you change," Melissa said. "There's a hair dryer in the bathroom if you want to dry your hair. Hurry, though. The spaghetti will be ready soon."

"Does your dad cook every night?" Lila asked.

"No, usually whoever's home first does it. Andy's got a part-time job, and Dad picks up odd jobs while he tries to sell the music he writes, so usually I'm the chef. But today Dad didn't have to work."

As Melissa started to shut the door, Lila's gaze fell on a worn photograph leaning against Melissa's dresser mirror.

"My mom," Melissa said softly.

"That's what I figured," Lila said. "She was really pretty, Melissa."

Melissa's eyes brimmed with tears. "She was beautiful," she whispered. "I miss her so much." Then she smiled. "I guess you and I have a little more in common than you'd think, huh?"

Lila nodded, thinking of how much she missed her own mother sometimes. She and Melissa *did* have things in common—more than Melissa ever would have guessed. For a moment, Lila considered telling Melissa her awful secret. She took a deep breath and opened her mouth to speak. But Melissa had already hurried off.

Lila felt a little bit better after she'd changed clothes and dried her hair. She glanced into the mirror in the bathroom and shook her head, smiling to herself. *If the Unicorns saw me now they probably wouldn't even recognize me*, she thought. She tossed her head proudly. *But even in these ratty old clothes, I still look pretty great!*

She was still smiling a few minutes later as she walked into the kitchen. "Hello, everyone," she said.

"I recognize that shirt," Andy exclaimed, looking up from the tray of garlic bread he was holding. "It used to be mine, until somebody I know shrank it—on purpose!"

"It was an accident!" Melissa cried. "Well, sort of," she added in a whisper to Lila.

"It's very comfortable," Lila said. She glanced down at the shirt with new interest now that she knew it had belonged to the star center of the Sweet Valley High basketball team.

"Here," Melissa said, handing a peeler to Lila. "Peel these carrots, OK?"

"What?" Lila asked distractedly, watching Mr. McCormick as he hustled back and forth between the stove and the refrigerator.

Melissa laughed. "I get the feeling Lila's never seen a man wearing an apron before, Dad."

"I take it your dad doesn't do a lot of cooking, Lila?" Mr. McCormick asked.

"Well, no," Lila said. "We have a house-keeper, Mrs. Pervis, who cooks for us. In fact she hates it when we go in the kitchen at all."

"Then you're missing all the fun!" Mr. McCormick exclaimed as he filled a pot with water.

"And all the cleanup," Melissa added. She passed Lila a handful of carrots.

Lila stood by the counter holding the carrots while Mr. McCormick, Andy, and Melissa dashed about the tiny, warm kitchen.

Lila stared from the peeler in her hand to a carrot and back again. It had never really occurred to her that carrots needed peeling. She tentatively scraped the peeler down the side of the carrot, but nothing happened. After a few more tries, she turned to Andy.

"There's something wrong with your peeler," she said.

Andy took one look and laughed. "You're holding the peeler upside down," he said. "Here." He reached over and demonstrated on a fresh car-rot, giving Lila a perfect view of his deep green eyes. "Lissa," Andy said, "I think we may actu-ally have discovered someone who's a worse cook than you."

Everyone laughed—even Lila, after Andy gave her a very nice smile.

Dinner turned out to be wonderful. "You're

almost as good a cook as Mrs. Pervis," Lila told Mr. McCormick as she held out her plate for a second helping of spaghetti.

"High praise, indeed," Mr. McCormick said.

"I kind of like eating in the kitchen like this," Lila said. "We always sit at this formal table in the dining room. My dad sits at one end and I sit at the other. I practically need binoculars to see him."

"Well, you're welcome to join us anytime," Mr. McCormick said.

"As long as you don't try to do any cooking," Andy added with a laugh.

After dinner, Lila helped Melissa do the dishes. By this time, she was beginning to feel right at home with the McCormicks. It was a relief to listen to them laugh and joke and to forget about her own problems for a while.

When the kitchen was cleaned up, the girls joined Andy and Mr. McCormick in the living room. Melissa brought her father his guitar, and for the next hour he played songs for them.

For a while, Lila sat back in an old easy chair, listening to Mr. McCormick's deep, soothing voice while she let herself forget her worries. But just when she was really starting to relax, he played a sad song he'd written about a man who was down on his luck and lost everything he'd ever owned. While Lila listened to the words, she thought of her own father and tears formed in her eyes.

"It's just a song, honey," Mr. McCormick said gently as he strummed the last chord. "Just a made-up song."

"I know," Lila answered. But Lila knew that although the song might not be real, her problems definitely were.

"Where were you last night?" Jessica asked the next morning in the hallway before homeroom. "I tried to call you a zillion times."

Lila shrugged. "I was kind of busy."

"Busy, how?"

"It's a long story," Lila said, looking away. She hadn't told any of the Unicorns yet about her visit to Melissa's. No one would ever believe that Lila had gone to the McCormicks' house for dinner—let alone that she'd had a good time.

Jessica narrowed her eyes. "What kind of long story?"

"It's no big deal, Jess," Lila muttered. "I had dinner at Melissa McCormick's house, that's all."

"What?" Jessica asked skeptically. "You hardly know Melissa."

"I *said* it was a long story, Jessica," Lila hissed.

"What did you two do all night, trade fashion tips?"

"Just drop it, OK?"

"Was Andy there?"

Lila nodded. "We peeled carrots together."

"You peeled carrots with Andy McCormick?"

Jessica cried in amazement. "He's adorable! I am so jealous!"

"So why were you calling me, anyway?" Lila asked, hoping to change the subject.

"I had a great idea for the balloon banner," Jessica replied. "I wanted to tell you about it right away."

Lila sighed. The last thing she felt like talking about was the Fling.

"I was thinking," Jessica continued, "what if we just have the balloon banner say 'Unicorn Founding Fling,' and leave it at that? You know— simple, understated. We don't want to be gaudy."

"Jessica," Lila said irritably, "a huge purple balloon floating over your house *is* gaudy."

"But it was your idea," Jessica protested.

"Well, I'm starting to have second thoughts," Lila said.

"What do you mean, *second thoughts*?" Jessica demanded. "You mean you're not going to have a hot-air balloon after all?"

Lila looked away and didn't answer.

"Lila?" Jessica asked. "Are you OK?"

"It's just—" Lila hesitated. "It's just that I have a lot on my mind," she said at last. "With the preparations for the Fling and all.

"That reminds me," Jessica said. "Do you want to go to the mall after school? We still need to find our Fling outfits."

Lila swallowed past a hard lump in her

throat. *How am I going to get out of this?* she wondered frantically. She *lived* to shop. If she refused to go to the mall, Jessica definitely would realize something was wrong.

"Daddy said he might be bringing me back something gorgeous and outrageously expensive from New York," Lila lied. "Why would I even want to bother with the Valley Mall?"

Jessica's face fell. "You're so lucky, Lila. And so spoiled," she added with a wry grin.

"It's like I told you," Lila said with a nervous shrug. "It isn't easy being rich." *And it isn't going to be easy being poor, either,* she added to herself.

Lila knew that Jessica and the rest of the Unicorns would never be able to understand what it was like being poor. What would they think of her if they knew? she wondered. She wasn't sure she really wanted to know the answer to that question.

Of course, Lila reminded herself, Melissa would understand. She was poor herself, after all, and she and Lila were friends now, sort of. Melissa was the only person Lila knew whose family didn't have a lot of money, except for Mandy Miller. But Mandy was a Unicorn, and that made confiding in her out of the question. Melissa was Lila's only hope.

"Have you seen Melissa yet this morning?" Lila asked suddenly.

"You mean your new buddy?" Jessica said.

She shook her head. "I don't get it, Lila. After all, Melissa is Elizabeth's friend. I can't quite see what you two have in common."

More than you'd ever guess, Lila thought grimly as she headed down the hall.

A few minutes later, Lila caught up with Melissa in front of her locker.

"Hi, Lila," Melissa exclaimed. She reached into her backpack. "You left your socks at my house last night," she said with a smile, handing them over.

"Thanks." Lila stuffed the socks into her purse. "Do you think we could talk—someplace private?"

"How about the bench over there?" Melissa asked, pointing.

"No, I mean *really* private."

"Whatever you say," Melissa said as Lila led her down the hallway and out the door. "But the bell's going to ring soon, and I don't want to be late to homeroom."

"It won't take long," Lila promised. She waited until they were halfway across the school lawn before she said anything more.

"I have to talk to someone," she finally blurted out. "I was talking to Jessica just now, and I started telling more lies—"

"Lies?"

"And I figured maybe you'd understand, because you're, well, you know—the P-word."

"P-word?" Melissa repeated. "You mean pretty?" she asked with a grin. "No? OK. How about perky? Pot-bellied?"

"Poor!" Lila shouted. As soon as the word was out of her mouth, she spun around to make sure no one had heard her.

"Oh, not that again," Melissa said, shaking her head. "You're so hung up on money, Lila. It's just not that big a deal."

"It is, if you have tons of it," Lila said, suddenly sniffling. "And then you . . . and then you don't anymore."

"Lila, what are you babbling about?"

"Do you promise not to tell, no matter who tries to drag it out of you? Especially Jessica—she can really be sneaky about that kind of thing."

Melissa laughed. "I promise."

Lila let out a deep, shuddery sigh. "My dad's broke."

Melissa frowned. "Are you sure?"

"Positive. I heard him with my very own ears. In fact, you were with me—that time in the hall. Remember how angry he sounded?"

"You said that was his business voice."

"It is. But he also said he'd lost a fortune."

"Oh that." Melissa gave a little wave of her hand. "I heard him say that. But that doesn't prove anything, Lila. It's just an expression."

Lila shook her head. "There's more evidence, though."

"Such as?"

"He refused to rent me a purple hot-air balloon."

Melissa still didn't seem convinced. "And?"

"And he fired our chauffeur."

"Randall? I thought he had beriberi."

Lila scowled. "I don't even know what beriberi *is*, Melissa. But trust me, Randall doesn't have it."

Melissa crossed her arms over her chest. "So that's it? That's all your evidence?"

"Don't you believe me?"

"I'm just not sure you've proved your case," Melissa said doubtfully. "Besides, if your father were in real financial trouble, don't you think he'd tell you?"

"Melissa, Melissa, Melissa," Lila said, shaking her head. "Rich people aren't like other people."

"Oh, really?"

"They hide their feelings and suffer in silence."

"I see," Melissa said. "Well, maybe you should ask your dad directly. Talk to him. It could be that you're worrying for nothing."

Lila shook her head. "He obviously doesn't want me to know yet—he's probably afraid I'll be totally overcome by the news. Anyway, I know I'm right, Melissa. And that's why I had to talk to you. You're the only person I know who wouldn't care about me being poor." She sighed.

"What am I going to do? If the Unicorns find out about this, they'll kick me out for sure."

"I doubt that—"

"—and they're definitely going to find out when I have to cancel the Founding Fling," Lila added frantically. "I'll be the laughingstock of the whole school." She chewed on her bottom lip. "Without money, I'm a big, fat nobody."

"Is that what you think of me and my family, Lila? That we're big, fat nobodies?" Melissa asked.

"Well, I used to," Lila admitted. "But now that I know you—"

"There, you see?" Melissa said firmly. "Even you must realize that money has nothing to do with the kind of person you really are."

"It has *everything* to do with the kind of person *I* am," Lila said seriously.

"Well, that's got to change," Melissa advised. "You have to stop thinking that the only reason people like you is because you have money. Do you really think the Unicorns would kick you out if they found out you weren't rich anymore?"

"Absolutely," Lila said.

Melissa laughed. "You know, Lila, I'm a little surprised to hear myself say this, but I like you. With or without money. And I'll bet the Unicorns would feel the same way."

Lila grabbed Melissa's arm and held on tightly. "Promise me you won't tell them!" she cried.

"I already promised," Melissa said as she

pried Lila's fingers loose. "Relax, Lila. Everything's going to be fine. You'll get through this."

"And you'll help me?"

"Sure."

"Good." Lila breathed a little sigh of relief. "Because I want you to be my poverty adviser."

"Your *what*?"

"You know. You can teach me how to act like regular people. Things like where the garbage goes when you take it out. And how to peel carrots."

"Important things," Melissa said, trying not to smile.

"Well, they didn't used to be important," Lila admitted. "But I guess they are now."

Melissa took Lila's hand and shook it. "Lila," she said with a grin, "I'd be happy to be your guide. Welcome to the real world."

Seven

That evening, Lila stood in the doorway to her father's study and took a deep breath. The door was open, and she could see him sitting in his big leather chair, bent over his desk. He had his calculator out, and there was a large pile of bills in front of him.

"Daddy?" she said quietly.

"Hmm?"

"Can I come in for a minute?"

Mr. Fowler looked over and smiled. "Sure, hon. But just for a minute, OK? I've got a ton of bills to pay here."

Lila sat down on the edge of the couch near his desk.

"So what can I do for my favorite daughter?" Mr. Fowler asked.

"I'm your *only* daughter," Lila reminded him.

She paused, trying to decide how to phrase her question. "I was just wondering . . . uh . . . how everything is."

"Everything?" Mr. Fowler repeated, his smile growing broader. "Could you be a little more specific?"

Lila hesitated. She wasn't used to talking to her father about serious things. And she couldn't just come right out and ask him if they were broke.

"You sure do have a lot of bills there," she said casually.

"*We* sure do have a lot of bills," Mr. Fowler corrected. He rummaged through the pile and retrieved one. "Was there some reason you felt the need to buy one hundred and fifty custom-made T-shirts at Silkscreen Specialties?" he asked, rubbing his temples. "In a variety of sizes, I might add. Are you planning on putting on a few pounds?"

"Those are souvenir T-shirts," Lila said defensively. "They all say 'I Flung at the Founding Fling' on the front. And on the back there's a picture of a purple unicorn. The Unicorns decided we needed souvenir T-shirts for all the guests— you know, like you can buy at rock concerts."

" 'I flung,' " Mr. Fowler repeated slowly.

"We weren't sure if it was 'I flung,' or 'I flinged,' " Lila admitted. "We spent an entire Unicorn meeting trying to decide."

"I see."

Lila shifted uncomfortably in her chair. Her father looked very tired. "I saved you a lot of money by getting those T-shirts, Daddy," she said.

"Oh?"

"I was going to get souvenir jackets for everybody, and you can just *imagine* how much those would have cost."

Mr. Fowler glanced at the bill again. "Your frugality is impressive, my dear," he said, but Lila had the feeling he wasn't entirely sincere.

"I could . . ." Lila hesitated. "I could return them, if you want."

"And what exactly is the store going to do with one hundred and fifty T-shirts that say 'I Flung at the Fling' on them?"

"The *Founding* Fling," Lila corrected.

Mr. Fowler sighed.

Lila looked down at her feet. This conversation wasn't going well at all. She glanced at her father and felt a sudden pang of worry. He really did look awfully tired.

"I love you, Daddy," she said suddenly. She got up and gave him a hug. "Everything will be OK."

"I love you, too," he said, looking a little surprised.

Lila walked back out into the hallway. Her father was too proud to say anything, but she knew now what she had to do. She'd avoided the inevitable long enough—she was going to have to cancel the Founding Fling. How could she spend all that money, knowing what her father was going through?

On Wednesday afternoon, Melissa and Elizabeth returned to the day-care center.

"I have a plan for the David mystery," Elizabeth said as she and Melissa were preparing sandwiches. "Why don't we follow him when he sneaks out after the snack break and see where he's going?"

Melissa smiled. "It's worth a try."

As soon as they had finished serving the snacks, Elizabeth took Melissa's arm and led her to the other side of the room. "We'll take turns watching him," she said. "Try not to look too obvious."

"Actually, I don't think we'll have to take too many turns," Melissa observed. "He's getting ready to go."

Elizabeth took a quick look over her shoulder and saw David once again sidling toward the back door. The little boy looked around cautiously, then swiftly ducked outside.

"After him," Elizabeth exclaimed.

The two girls raced across the room and outside, emerging just in time to see David disappear around the corner of the building.

"There," Elizabeth said, pointing.

They followed David as he rounded a corner, walked half a block, and bolted down a dark, dead-end alleyway. He didn't seem to notice them behind him as he hurried along, holding one hand protectively over the jacket pocket containing the peanut-butter-and-jelly sandwich he'd taken.

"Why would he head over here to play?" Melissa whispered as they walked along the alley, which was lined with trash cans piled high with refuse and littered with empty boxes.

Then they saw David stop. He was bending over something behind a pile of wooden crates. Something very furry.

"Here, boy," David said softly as he reached into his pocket and pulled out the sandwich.

"David?" Elizabeth called, taking a step closer.

David spun around in surprise, revealing the recipient of the peanut-butter-and-jelly sandwich—a large, reddish-brown, very dirty dog.

"Please don't take him away!" David wailed. "He's not hurting anybody!"

"It's OK," Melissa reassured him.

"Whose dog is this?" Elizabeth asked.

"He's mine," David said defiantly. "I've had Charlie since I was little."

"But what's he doing here in this alley?" Elizabeth asked.

David looked down at the ground. "He was

my dog when we had a house. My dad said we couldn't afford to keep him anymore. He said he was going to put Charlie in the dog pound."

"So how did he get here?" Melissa asked. She knelt down to scratch Charlie's ear.

"I told my dad he ran away," David admitted. "Right before we had to get out of our house. But I tied him up in my old neighborhood. Then, after we came here to the shelter, I went back and got him."

Elizabeth knelt down so she could talk to David face-to-face. "But David, you know you can't keep Charlie in this alley forever," she said gently.

"Someday we'll have a house of our own," David replied, thrusting out his chin. "My dad and me and Charlie. Just as soon as my dad gets a job."

"Yes, but that may take a while," Elizabeth said kindly.

"I can't just give Charlie away, can I? He would never give *me* away."

Elizabeth sighed and looked at Melissa. "He can't stay here," she said. "Someone's bound to call the pound and have him picked up eventually. And in the meantime, it's dangerous for David to keep sneaking out to this alley."

"Well, there's no way I'm going to be responsible for separating these two," Melissa said firmly. "I'd let Charlie stay at my house, but my brother is allergic to dogs. He breaks out in hives if he gets within fifty yards of one." She gazed at Elizabeth hopefully.

"Jessica doesn't really get along with dogs," Elizabeth said. "As a matter of fact, she *hates* them." She paused and a slow smile spread across her face. "Then again, maybe this would be a perfect way for Jessica to help out the center without taking time away from the Unicorns."

Melissa grinned. "I agree."

"I'll definitely have to break it to her slowly," Elizabeth said, gazing at Charlie thoughtfully. "Not to mention my parents. But, if it's only for a while . . ."

David was looking back and forth between Elizabeth and Melissa hopefully. "You mean Charlie can stay at your house until my dad gets a job?" he asked eagerly. "He won't have to stay in this smelly old alley anymore?"

Elizabeth nodded. She couldn't help smiling at David's happy expression. She was sure that her parents would agree to the plan when she explained it to them. But she wasn't so sure about Jessica.

"What exactly is that thing?"

"It's called a dog, Jess," Elizabeth said calmly as she led Charlie into the kitchen later that afternoon. "His name is Charlie."

"His name should be 'Disgusting,' " Jessica

said as she finished making a peanut-butter-and-jelly sandwich. "Why's his tongue hanging out like that?"

"That's how dogs sweat," Elizabeth replied.

Charlie loped over to Jessica and licked her hand.

"Go sweat on someone else, dog," she said, scowling. "What's the deal, Elizabeth? You're not actually going to try to get Mom and Dad to let you keep this monster, are you? Because if you are—"

"They already said yes," Elizabeth replied.

Charlie wagged his tail and licked Jessica's other hand.

"Stop slobbering on me!" Jessica commanded. "What do you mean, they said yes? They didn't even ask me."

Just then Steven entered the kitchen. "Jess, is that you?" he said, kneeling down to scratch Charlie's ears. "I really like what you've done with your hair." Charlie licked Steven's face.

"Shut up, Steven," Jessica said. "Anyway, you and Charlie deserve each other." She headed for the refrigerator. "Although Charlie's probably got a higher IQ than you do."

"I think he's got a crush on you, Jess," Steven said as Charlie ran over to give her another kiss.

"Well, don't get too attached, Charlie," Elizabeth warned. She looked at Jessica and Steven. "This is only temporary. Charlie belongs to a little boy at the homeless shelter's day-care center. I called Mom and Dad, and they said we could let Charlie stay here until his family finds a permanent home."

"Why couldn't you put him in the dog pound like a normal person?" Jessica demanded.

"Come on, Jessica," Elizabeth chided. "You said you cared about the underprivileged."

"Underprivileged *people*, not underprivileged *dogs*," Jessica replied.

"Why do you hate dogs so much, Jess?" Steven asked as he sat at the kitchen table.

"I don't hate dogs," Jessica said, pouring herself a glass of milk. "They hate me."

"Charlie seems to like you," Elizabeth pointed out. "And what about Mrs. Bramble's dog, Sally? You two ended up liking each other just fine in the end."

"That was different. I was getting paid to get along with Sally." Jessica started to return the milk carton to the refrigerator, but Charlie was still underfoot. "Stop slobbering all over me, will you?" She pointed to the other side of the kitchen. "Go," she said firmly. "Go over there."

Charlie hung his head. Slowly he walked away in the direction she was pointing, his tail between his legs. "That's better," Jessica said as she put the milk away. Behind her she heard Elizabeth's and Steven's muffled laughter.

"What's so funny?" she demanded, spinning around.

Steven shrugged.

"Don't look at me," Elizabeth said. "I'm just an innocent bystander."

Jessica put her hands on her hips. "I just have one thing to say. I don't want to have anything to do with this drooling mutt while he's here, understand? I'm not taking him for walks, or brushing him, or playing with him, or feeding—"

Suddenly she stopped short. "Who took my sandwich?" she demanded.

Elizabeth, Steven, and Charlie all stared at her with wide, innocent eyes.

"What was that you were saying about feeding Charlie?" Steven asked with a smirk.

"You ate my sandwich?" Jessica cried, glaring at Charlie.

Elizabeth shrugged. "I guess I forgot to mention that he loves peanut butter and jelly."

"See what I mean?" Jessica cried. "This is why I hate dogs! They can't be trusted. They have fleas, and they bark at the mailman, and they sweat with their tongues." She put her hands on her hips and scowled at Charlie, who wagged his tail hopefully. "And they steal your food."

"Come on, Jess," Steven urged. "When's the last time a guy this cute followed you around and drooled all over you?"

"Forget it, Steven," Jessica said. "I do not like dogs, and dogs do not like me."

Charlie wagged his tail hopefully, his brown eyes on Jessica. "Trust me," Jessica warned. "You're wasting your time, you mangy old mutt."

Eight

"Lesson number one," Melissa said. "Only buy what you really need."

"What I really need," Lila repeated thoughtfully as the girls walked through the mall. It was Saturday afternoon, and the stores were packed with shoppers.

"Lesson number two," Melissa continued. "Only buy things that are on sale."

"On sale," Lila echoed. She paused in front of a window to admire a pair of shoes.

"Come on, Lila," Melissa warned, tugging on her arm.

"But they're so cute!" Lila moaned.

"Do you need them?"

Lila hesitated.

"Lila, tell the truth. Don't you already have a pair of shoes almost exactly like that?"

"Mine are brown, Melissa," Lila argued.

"So are the ones in the window."

"The ones in the window are *dark* brown," Lila replied.

Melissa pursed her lips. "Do you have any aspirin, Lila?"

"Do you have a headache?"

"Not yet," Melissa said with a sigh. "But I have a feeling I'm going to." She yanked Lila away from the window.

"Where are you taking me?"

"To Driscoll's Discount Store."

Lila groaned. "How humiliating. What if someone sees me?"

Melissa pointed toward Driscoll's, a large store at the end of the mall. "You asked me to be your poverty adviser," she said sternly. "So take my advice—get moving."

Lila put her hand on her forehead. "You know, I'm feeling a little lightheaded. Maybe we should try this another day."

"That's what you said yesterday when we went to the drug store. But you bought generic shampoo and lived to tell about it, didn't you?"

Lila nodded. "But I'm sure people were talking about me behind my back."

Melissa stared at the floor, trying not to smile. "Well, I didn't want to tell you this, Lila, but there *was* a report on the evening news about it."

"Fine!" Lila exclaimed. "Make fun of me when I'm down and out, Melissa!"

Melissa grinned. By now she'd learned that joking with Lila was the best way to handle her. "Come on, let's go. Driscoll's awaits."

The girls began threading their way through the crowd. "Look at that dress," Lila exclaimed as they passed a purple dress in a window display. "That would have been perfect for the Fling." She looked sad. "I never realized how hard it is not to have much money," she confessed in a whisper as they moved past the window. "I already miss being able to buy things I want. How do you stand it, Melissa?"

Melissa smiled. "I'd rather be happy than be rich, wouldn't you?"

"I'd rather be both," Lila replied, gazing back longingly at the dress in the window.

Melissa turned and looked at Lila seriously as they walked into Driscoll's. "You know, you're going to have to tell people something about the Fling soon," she said gently. "You can't let things go on too much longer. There'll be the caterers to cancel, and the band—"

"I know," Lila interrupted. "But I haven't figured out how to do it yet. I just need a little more time. Every time I try to imagine telling the Unicorns, I picture the looks of horror on their faces." She paused. "They're going to hate me, you know."

"No, they're not. They're your friends, and friends stick by you, rich or poor." Melissa stopped in front of a table stacked high with sweaters. "Now, here's a good buy. Thirty percent off." She examined a price tag. "And see? They've been marked down twice."

Lila shook her head. "I guess I'm just not a bargain kind of person."

"Too bad," Melissa said thoughtfully. "Because if you were, you could put on a great bargain Fling. You know, you really don't need tons of cash to throw a great party."

"*I* do," Lila said.

"Seriously, Lila. I could help you. That way you could still have the Fling."

"Forget it," Lila said with a wave of her hand. "There's no way—" Suddenly she froze. "Oh no, look!" she cried, pointing across the store. "It's Elizabeth and Jessica!"

"So?"

"*So?* So hide!" Lila cried as she dove under the table.

"Lila," Melissa exclaimed, peeking under the table. "You're being ridiculous."

"Hi, Melissa," Elizabeth called. "We're here buying a leash for Charlie."

"How's he doing?"

"Great," Elizabeth answered. "Jessica, I'm not so sure about. Charlie's madly in love with her."

"And I have the dog drool all over me to prove it," Jessica complained. She glanced around her. "I know this sounds crazy, but didn't I just see Lila here?"

"Lila?" Melissa repeated evasively. "What would Lila be doing here?"

"You're right," Jessica said. "Lila wouldn't be caught dead in a store like this."

Melissa glanced down at the floor. Lila was well hidden under the table, but her purple purse was sticking out. Melissa gave the purse a little nudge with her toe.

"Ow!" Lila cried.

"I thought that was your purse," Melissa hissed. She smiled sheepishly at Jessica and Elizabeth. "You may as well come out, Lila."

"All right, all right," Lila grumbled.

Jessica peered under the table. "Taking inventory, Lila?"

"I was just helping Melissa shop," Lila muttered as she struggled out from under the table. "And I dropped my purse."

Jessica narrowed her eyes. "Melissa asked you to help her shop?"

"Well, I *am* an expert," Lila replied haughtily.

"Lila," Melissa said, giving her a meaningful look. "Don't you think maybe it's time—"

"Time?" Lila interrupted quickly, glancing at her gold watch. "You're absolutely right, Melissa. I almost forgot. Daddy and I have an appointment with the balloon people this afternoon."

"Lila!" Melissa cried.

"I know, I know. I promised to help you work on your fashion sense." She grabbed a black sweater off the table and tossed it to Melissa. "Here," she called over her shoulder as she dashed away. "Buy this one. You can't go wrong with basic black."

Without another word, she disappeared into the crowd.

"What do you mean, *Lila's broke?*" Jessica cried in disbelief a few minutes later.

"Quiet, Jessica," Melissa said sharply as she and the twins sat down at a table in the food court.

"Lila Fowler, broke?" Jessica shook her head. "It just isn't possible."

"Keep your voice down," Melissa warned. "You promised you'd keep this a secret." She sighed. "I feel terrible about breaking my promise by telling you this, but Lila's making herself miserable pretending everything's the same as always. When I saw her hide under the table at Driscoll's, I realized that things were getting out of hand. I just felt I had to tell you. After all, you are her closest friend."

"I think you did the right thing, Melissa," Elizabeth said. "Maybe together we can come up with some way to help Lila."

"If only I'd known," Jessica moaned. "I keep thinking about the way we teased her over that stupid credit card. Poor Lila."

"The problem is, Lila thinks no one will like her anymore once they know she's broke," Melissa said.

"That's crazy!" Jessica cried. "I'll admit that having a rich best friend does have advantages. But I like Lila for her personality. She's—" Jessica hesitated.

"—nice?" Melissa offered.

"Well, no, not exactly," Jessica admitted.

"—funny?" Elizabeth suggested.

Jessica shook her head. "Not usually. Although that stunt under the sale table was pretty hilarious."

"How about generous?" Melissa ventured.

"Nope. Lila's really pretty stingy, unless she's giving a party where she can be the center of attention."

The three girls sat silently for a moment.

"OK," Jessica said at last. "So it's kind of hard to explain why I like Lila. She's just, well, *Lila*. And there's no one else quite like her."

"Thank goodness for that," Melissa said with a laugh. "I don't think I could take more than one of her."

"So what do you think we should do?" Jessica asked.

"I keep trying to convince her to tell everyone

the truth," Melissa said. "She knows she's going to have to cancel the Fling, but she can't figure out how to break it to everyone."

"Too bad about that," Jessica said unhappily. She tried to imagine the Unicorns' faces when they heard the news. It was not going to be a pretty sight. Jessica sighed. "I was really looking forward to the Fling, too."

"Jessica," Elizabeth said, "try to put yourself in Lila's place."

"The important thing is to be as understanding and supportive as possible," Melissa said.

"Just be a good friend," Elizabeth advised.

"I'll try," Jessica vowed.

"And don't breathe a word of this to anyone," Melissa warned, staring intently at Jessica.

"Not a soul," Jessica promised, not meeting her eyes. *Not unless I really have to*, she added silently.

"I hereby call this secret emergency meeting of the Unicorns to order," Janet announced on Sunday afternoon.

All the Unicorns except Lila were assembled in Jessica's bedroom. Janet was sitting in Jessica's desk chair, while the rest of the girls were sitting on the bed or sprawled on the carpet.

Janet looked over at Jessica. "Since Jessica called this meeting, maybe she could fill us all in now on what the big secret emergency is."

Jessica got to her feet and waited until everyone had fallen silent. For a moment, she wondered if she were doing the right thing. After all, if Lila wanted the Unicorns to know about this, she would have told them herself. But Lila was too proud for that, Jessica reminded herself. And the Unicorns couldn't help her if they didn't know about her problem. It was Jessica's duty as her best friend to spill the beans. The important thing was to break the news to the Unicorns gradually, so they wouldn't be too upset.

"This is going to be the most unbelievable thing any of you have ever heard," she began, pacing the floor. "You're going to be shocked. I guarantee it. In fact, I think this may be the most important Unicorn meeting we've ever held."

"Does it involve Lila?" Ellen interrupted.

"Of course it involves Lila," Mandy said. "Why else would Jessica ask us not to tell Lila what was going on?"

"Yeah, what's the big mystery that we can't tell Lila?" Kimberly said. "It's kind of weird having to keep a meeting secret from one of our own members."

"Is Lila sick or something?" Grace Oliver asked.

"If you'll all shut up, I'll tell you what's going on," Jessica said in an exasperated voice. "Now, as I was saying before I was so rudely interrupted, this is something of earth-shattering importance—"

"Lila's quitting the Unicorns!" Ellen cried.

"Lila's moving to another city," Betsy Gordon guessed.

"Lila's running away from home," Belinda said.

Jessica threw up her hands. "No, no, no!" she shouted. "Lila's *broke!*"

She was gratified when a long silence followed.

"She *can't* be broke," Tamara said at last. "Everybody knows Lila is rich."

"Not anymore." Jessica shook her head sadly. "Her dad lost his fortune in a business deal and now he's broke. They've already fired the chauffeur and they may have to move out of their house into a tiny apartment." She took a deep breath. "She's even going to have to cancel the Fling."

"Cancel the Fling?" Tamara echoed.

"We're not Flinging?" Ellen cried.

"How do you know all this, Jessica?" Janet demanded.

"Melissa McCormick told me," Jessica said.

"How would *she* know?"

"Lila told her."

"Lila told Melissa?" Janet exclaimed incredulously. "Since when does Lila hang around with Melissa? Melissa isn't a Unicorn."

"Not even close," Ellen put in snidely.

"Lila told Melissa because she thought she could give her pointers," Jessica explained. "Melissa is teaching Lila to be poor."

Ellen shrugged. "Why would anyone want to take poor lessons?"

"You know," Janet said, ignoring Ellen, "I should have realized something was up when Lila's credit card got refused. That was a sign."

"Plus there was the thing about Randall," Mandy pointed out. "Who ever heard of beriberi, anyway?"

"Well, why didn't she come to us with her problem?" Mary Wallace asked. "We're her friends. She knows she can count on the Unicorns."

"She's obviously been trying to keep it a secret," Belinda said.

Grace nodded. "Probably because she's so embarrassed."

"It's more than that," Jessica said grimly. "Melissa told me that Lila's afraid we won't like her anymore if she's not rich."

"Of course we'll still like her!" Ellen cried. She paused, looking slightly confused. "Won't we?"

"*Yes*, Ellen," Jessica said sternly. "You shouldn't even have to ask." She rubbed her chin thoughtfully. "Now, here's the thing. We can't let Lila know we've found out about her money problems."

"That's easy," Belinda said. "Everyone should just act normal."

"That means no more teasing," Jessica said.

"Not at all?" Kimberly asked.

"Nope. And whatever you do, don't ask her to pay for anything."

"She never pays for anything anyway," Ellen said. "Lila's really pretty cheap, when you get right down to it."

"We should try being extra nice to her, too," Mandy suggested.

"Poor Lila," Mary Wallace said. "She's probably so worried about the party. I wish there were some way we could make this easier for her."

"Maybe there is," Jessica exclaimed. "What if we all chipped in and helped out with the party? That way she wouldn't have to cancel it. We could make decorations—"

"And food," Betsy added.

"That's a great idea," Janet cried. "I'll be in charge. We'll call it—Operation Fling! We'll show up the day the Fling was supposed to be and surprise her."

"Don't forget, though," Jessica warned. "Nobody breathe a word of this to Lila. No matter what, we can't let her suspect a thing!"

Nine

"No, no, *you* go first, Lila," Janet said as they stood in line together in the school cafeteria on Monday.

Lila stepped forward, eyeing Janet suspiciously. "I'm just getting a milk, anyway," Lila said, trying to conceal the brown paper bag in her hand.

Once she got to the Unicorner, though, there was no way to hide the fact that she was eating a lunch Mrs. Pervis had made for her that morning. Lila had never brought a brown bag lunch to school in her entire life. She took a deep breath and set the bag on the table beside her milk.

For a moment, the Unicorns all fell perfectly silent, staring at the bag in disbelief.

With burning cheeks, Lila unwrapped her sandwich and stole a glance around the table. All eyes were glued to her tuna fish on whole wheat.

"I, uh, I just got tired of the same boring

cafeteria food all the time," Lila muttered. "You can only stand so much mystery meat."

"I *absolutely* agree," Jessica said, nodding vigorously.

"Me, too," Belinda said with a smile.

"You are *so* right, Lila," Janet said, pushing her tray away from her. "I think I'll start brown-bagging it too. A person could get food poisoning from the stuff they try to pass off as food in this place."

"This lasagna is gross!" Ellen yelled suddenly, spitting a mouthful of food out on her tray. "It's the worst stuff I've ever eaten in my whole life!"

All heads turned to stare at Ellen.

Ellen shrugged sheepishly, and Lila noticed Jessica rolling her eyes toward the ceiling.

"You know, I was thinking," Janet began. "Not for any reason or anything, just thinking, you know? And what I was thinking was that it's the little things in life that are really important."

"Uh-huh," Lila said between bites of sandwich.

"See, it's not how big something is that's important," Janet said philosophically.

"Oh, I agree," Mary said. "Sometimes things can get so big that they just get to be *too* much, you know?"

"Good things come in small packages," Mandy said.

Lila looked at her doubtfully.

"My grandmother always says that," Mandy added lamely.

"She means things like jewelry," Lila said. "Jewelry always comes in small boxes."

"No! Not jewelry," Mandy exclaimed in a horrified voice. "Who said anything about jewelry? You know me—I never wear jewelry."

Lila raised her eyebrows and glanced at the chunky purple bracelet on Mandy's wrist and the three strands of beads around her neck. Once again everyone grew quiet.

"So anyway," Janet began after a pause, "what I was thinking was how we sometimes get carried away with, you know, *things*."

"All of us," Jessica said solemnly.

"I know *I* do," Tamara said.

"*All* of us," Janet repeated. "Every one of us gets carried away with making things too big and, um, expensive."

"We shouldn't do that," Mandy agreed. "We should keep things simple."

"That's exactly right," Janet confirmed.

"What do *you* think about that, Lila?" Mary asked.

"About what?" Lila asked.

"About small things being better," Janet prompted.

Lila shrugged. "Whatever you say." She pointed to the untouched apple pie on Janet's tray. "Are you going to eat that? Mrs. Pervis didn't pack me a dessert."

"No, *you* eat it," Janet said quickly. "I'm not hungry."

"Take mine, too," Mandy suggested. "I'm going on a diet. I just decided."

"I've only eaten half my pie," Ellen added. "Here, Lila. You can have the rest."

Lila gazed around the table in exasperation. The Unicorns were definitely acting strange today. She couldn't help wondering if they'd somehow caught on to her secret. But that wasn't possible, she reassured herself. The only person who knew about her was Melissa, and Melissa barely even knew the Unicorns.

Lila cleared her throat. "Am I going crazy, or is something going on with all of you?"

Suddenly, everyone seemed very interested in examining their lunches. No one would meet Lila's eyes.

"Because," Lila continued, "it sure seems like we've been having a very weird conversation."

"Nope. Normal," Janet said briskly. "Wouldn't you say so, Jessica?"

"Seems normal to me," Jessica agreed.

"Definitely normal," Ellen added.

"Well, everyone's been talking about what they've been thinking. We don't usually talk about—you know, *thoughts*. It's weird."

"No one's been thinking anything weird," Janet said with a little laugh.

"Janet's right," Belinda said quickly.

Ellen leaned across the table. "I can promise you, Lila," she said very seriously, "I haven't been thinking anything at all. And I never will."

Lila forced a smile. Somehow, she wasn't reassured.

"Melissa, I'm sorry about the way I acted on Saturday," Lila said on Monday afternoon as the two girls walked home from school. "It's just that I was so embarrassed when I saw Jessica coming. I mean, those sweaters were *polyester!*"

"It's OK, Lila, really," Melissa said. "But I do think you've got to start facing facts. You can't go on forever pretending nothing's changed."

Lila sighed. "I know you're right. But I just can't bear the thought of how everyone's going to react when they find out I'm not rich anymore." She shook her head. "You know, it's kind of funny. It's not really losing the money I'm worried about the most. Sure, I'll miss the big parties. And the designer clothes." She sighed. "And the limo rides to school. And the front-row seats at rock concerts. And the weekend trips to Hawaii. And the gold jewelry—"

"Is there a *but* in here somewhere?" Melissa interrupted.

"What? Oh, yeah. But I'll miss my friends in the Unicorns most of all."

"There's no reason for you to think you're going to lose them," Melissa said.

"They're already acting strange," Lila replied. She stopped to rub her foot. "Can we slow down a little? I've got major blisters from walking so much. Randall may have been a jerk, but I sure do miss him."

Melissa paused next to Lila. "What do you mean about the Unicorns acting strange?"

"Today I brought my lunch to school, just like you taught me," Lila said. "And they were acting really weird at the Unicorner. It's almost as if they suspect me or something. Unicorns are that way," she added. "They have loser detectors in their brains."

Melissa cleared her throat. "I'm sure they don't suspect anything, Lila. That's crazy. But they *are* going to find out eventually. The party's only a few days away. If you're going to cancel it, you can't wait much longer."

"I know." Lila chewed on her bottom lip. "I guess I could start by calling the caterers and stuff, then work my way up to the Unicorns. This would be a good time to do it, since my dad's out of town again for a few days. When he gets home, I could give him the news that I'd just saved him zillions of dollars." She sighed. "It will make me feel a little better to know I'm helping him out. I'll bet this is even tougher on him than it has been on me."

"I still say you could give a great party without spending tons of cash," Melissa argued. "Andy and I have done it."

"I'm sure your parties were nice and everything, Melissa. But you can't compare them to the Founding Fling I had planned."

"Oh, yeah?" Melissa asked, hands on her hips. "I'll bet that you and I could put on the party of a lifetime without spending much money at all."

"I suppose you believe in the Tooth Fairy, too."

"Come on, Lila! Don't you want to have the Fling?"

"Yes, but only if it's the best one in the history of the Unicorns."

"If we worked hard enough, it still could be!"

"But without the hot-air balloon and the luau and the live band, how could it be any fun?"

Melissa smiled. "It is actually possible to have fun without spending tons of money, Lila."

"I wouldn't know. I've never tried."

"Look," Melissa said. "The way I see it, you have two choices. Have your party my way, or don't have it at all. Either way, everyone's going to find out the truth."

Lila pursed her lips. She knew Melissa was right. The idea of giving a bargain party was awfully hard to swallow. But wasn't a cheap party better than no party at all?

"Well, if I'm going to be socializing like a poor person from now on, I guess throwing a cheapo Fling would be a good way to practice. Would you help me with it?" Lila said at last.

"On one condition."

"What's that?"

"That you agree to volunteer at the shelter day-care center with Elizabeth and me."

"Oh, please!" Lila moaned. "Don't you think I'm suffering enough already?"

"The offer stands," Melissa said. "Come on, just give it a try."

"OK, OK, if it means that much to you. But don't expect me to *enjoy* it or anything."

"Great!" Melissa said. "I promise you that you won't be sorry."

"About the shelter or about the party?"

"Either one."

"I hope you're right." Lila sighed. "What's the worst that can happen if I give a cheap party?" She waved her hand. "Cancel that question. I already know. The worst that can happen is that the Unicorns will never forgive me."

On Tuesday morning, Jessica woke up hugging her favorite old stuffed teddy bear, Fuzzy.

"Hello, Fuzzy," she murmured, cuddling against his soft warm fur. She could hear Elizabeth brushing her teeth in the bathroom, and the smell of breakfast was drifting up from downstairs. It was time to get up, she knew, but she felt so cozy that she hated to get out of bed.

She closed her eyes a little tighter and rubbed her face against Fuzzy's long, soft fur.

Suddenly she remembered something. She hadn't slept with Fuzzy in years. Mrs. Wakefield had thrown him in the washer and his stuffing had exploded. Fuzzy was dead.

So who, exactly, was licking her face?

"Aargh!" Jessica screamed as her eyes flew open. She flung back the covers and leapt out of bed.

Charlie leapt out of bed, too, wagging his tail happily.

"Jess?" Elizabeth cried, opening the door to the bathroom that connected their two rooms.

"He was in my bed!" Jessica cried. "His disgusting dog lips were on my pillow!"

"And you said you didn't get along with dogs," Elizabeth said, laughing.

Jessica began yanking her sheets off her bed. "These sheets will have to be burned!" she exclaimed.

Charlie grabbed one end of a sheet in his mouth and began playing tug-of-war. "Stop it," Jessica moaned. "Elizabeth, make him stop!" She turned to her twin for support, but Elizabeth was laughing too hard to be of much help.

"Stop it, Charlie," Jessica commanded as she

pulled as hard as she could on the sheet. "I mean it!"

Suddenly Charlie let go of the sheet, and Jessica went tumbling backward. She landed in a heap on the floor at the foot of her bed. Charlie galloped over and leapt on top of her, wagging his tail so hard that his whole rear end wiggled.

"Charlie," Jessica said in a resigned tone, staring up at the furry face above her. "Don't you understand? I hate dogs. You're a dog. This relationship is not going to work out. Besides, this is no way to wake me up in the morning."

Elizabeth reached over and stroked Charlie's head. She grinned at Jessica. "Tomorrow morning maybe you should try just setting your alarm."

Ten

◇

"I believe I may be witnessing a miracle," Elizabeth said in amazement on Wednesday afternoon. "An actual miracle."

"Now, pretend you don't know anything," Melissa said tersely. "Act like you would normally."

"That may be difficult under the circumstances," Elizabeth said. "Seeing Lila Fowler volunteer for something is not exactly your normal event."

"Well, it did take me a while to convince her to come," Melissa said.

"Hi, you two," Lila called out when she caught sight of them.

"Lila?" Elizabeth said. "Is that really you under there? I mean, blue jeans and a sweatshirt? I didn't know you *owned* a sweatshirt!"

"I didn't want people to think I was showing

off," Lila said guardedly. "So I wore something poor." She looked at Elizabeth's outfit. "What's your excuse?"

Melissa laughed. Somehow it was reassuring to see that Lila was still her usual blunt, obnoxious self.

Before Elizabeth could respond, Connie joined the group. "So, what have we here?" she asked. "A new volunteer?"

"I've come to help those less fortunate," Lila said earnestly.

"I'm sure 'those less fortunate' will appreciate your help," Connie said wryly. "Do you have any experience with children? Say, baby-sitting?"

Lila considered for a moment. "No, I've never been around little kids. But I know how to peel carrots."

Connie sent a confused glance in Melissa's direction. Melissa just shrugged.

"I'll certainly keep your carrot skills in mind," Connie said at last. "In the meantime, maybe Melissa and Elizabeth could show you the ropes. They know their way around pretty well."

"Thank you," Lila said politely as Connie walked away, chuckling under her breath.

"Come on, Lila," Elizabeth said. "We'll show you something *really* fun. We call it *cleaning the bathroom.*"

"Cleaning the bathroom?" Lila scowled. "I thought we were here to do good deeds."

"This *is* a good deed. You can do the mirrors," Melissa said as she handed Lila some glass cleaner and a roll of paper towels. "If you do well enough, we may be able to promote you to the sink. With a little practice, you'll be ready for the toilet soon."

While the girls were cleaning the bathroom, David walked over to watch them. "How's Charlie?" he asked shyly.

"He's doing great," Elizabeth assured him. "But he misses you a lot."

"Not as much as I miss him," David murmured. He hesitated, staring at his dirty sneakers. "You don't think he'll start liking your family better because you have a nice house, do you?"

Elizabeth patted David on the shoulder. "Not a chance. As far as Charlie's concerned, it's just a temporary stay in a dog hotel."

"You sure?"

"Positive."

David stood up a little straighter. "My dad'll get a job soon," he vowed, "and then Charlie can come live in *our* house."

"We'll keep our fingers crossed," Elizabeth said.

"And our toes," Melissa added.

David smiled and ran back to join the other children in the playroom.

"Poor kid," Lila said softly as she watched him leave. "It must be hard to lose everything like that—" Suddenly she broke off and began scrubbing the mirror with extra energy. "So what do you guys have lined up for me next?" she demanded in a thick voice. "Think I'm ready for toilet duty?"

Melissa hesitated. She could tell Lila was feeling sad, but there was nothing she could say—not now, in front of Elizabeth.

"Let's skip the toilets and go straight to diapers," she said finally, trying to sound upbeat. She led Lila to the three cribs that were arranged together at one end of the playroom. Two of the babies were fast asleep, while the third played contentedly with a rattle.

"You're lucky," Melissa said. "So far no one needs changing."

Lila looked nervously at the babies. "Couldn't I just volunteer for certain things? I'll need more training before I can handle something as complicated as diapers. Besides, cleaning those mirrors kind of wore me out."

"I suppose we could take it easy on you this first time," Melissa said, smiling. "This would be a good time to read the kids a story."

"A story?" Lila asked. "I can handle that."

Melissa and Elizabeth watched as Lila went over to the reading corner, which was furnished with old bean bag chairs and throw pillows. Several children gathered around her immediately.

"We already read *that* one," Sara said as Lila held up a book.

Lila pulled out a second book.

"Nope." Janie shook her head.

After three more unsuccessful tries, Lila slumped down on one of the pillows, looking dejected. For a moment she stared out the window. Then she sat up, forcing herself to smile. "I've got an idea," she said. "I'll tell you a new story."

"Which story?" David asked skeptically.

"A story about—" she paused. "About a princess who lived in a magical castle until her father, the king, lost his job."

Melissa and Elizabeth exchanged knowing glances.

"How come he lost his job?" John asked.

"I'm sure it wasn't his fault," Lila said. "It was just one of those things."

"Was the princess sad?" Sara asked.

"You better believe it," Lila replied. "She was used to wearing a diamond crown and beautiful designer gowns. And all of a sudden she had to get used to wearing, uh, blue jeans. Plus, she didn't have a cook anymore. She had to learn to make carrots and peanut-butter sandwiches." Lila sighed. "For a while, as I'm sure you can imagine, she was really bummed out."

"Did she cry?" David asked softly.

Lila looked over at him and smiled. "At first she did. But then—" she paused, "then she realized that it was more important to be happy than to be rich. And that made her feel a whole lot better. Most of the time, anyway."

Lila stopped talking and stared out the window. For a moment, the children were quiet.

"So what happened to the princess?" Janie asked at last, sounding a little impatient. "Did she live happily ever after?"

"I wish I knew," Lila answered wistfuly. "I'll have to tell you the rest another day. I don't know the ending of the story yet."

"So what should we say on the banner?" Jessica asked that afternoon. All the Unicorns except Lila were gathered at the Wakefields' house to work on Operation Fling.

"I don't see why we need a banner if we're not going to have a balloon," Ellen complained.

Jessica began unfolding a white sheet and spreading it across the kitchen floor over a layer of newspapers. "We're going to hang it above the front door of Lila's house," she explained. "It's not as eye-catching as a balloon, but it'll have to do."

"We don't have a lot of room," Mandy said as she opened a small can of bright purple paint, "or a lot of paint. Maybe we should just say 'Welcome to the Founding Fling,' and leave it at that."

"How about 'Welcome to Lila Fowler's Founding Fling'?" Mary suggested.

"And not even mention *us*?" Ellen cried.

"Ellen," Belinda reminded her, "we're supposed to be helping Lila in her time of need."

"Sorry," Ellen said quietly. "I forgot. It's kind of hard to think of Lila as needy."

"This meeting is totally out of control," Janet interrupted, pounding on the kitchen table. "If Operation Fling is going to be a success, someone has to organize it. Now, I think what we need are committees. We'll have a cooking committee to come up with food, an entertainment committee, and a decorations committee."

Mandy and Jessica had started to paint on the sheet as Ellen watched.

"Your 'W' is a little crooked, Jess," Ellen said helpfully.

"Put Ellen on the cooking committee, will you, Janet?" Jessica suggested, giving Ellen a dirty look.

"What will we do if Lila tells everyone the party's canceled?" Grace asked, picking up a brush to help Jessica and Mandy paint.

"She won't," Jessica said confidently. "Melissa told me that she convinced Lila to try to put on the party cheaply."

"Lila put on a cheap party?" Betsy exclaimed. "No way!"

"It's true," Jessica said. "The other day I saw them at the dime store buying paper streamers and stuff."

"But Lila's never done anything cheaply in her life," Tamara pointed out.

"Melissa's training her," Jessica said.

"Maybe we should just tell Lila that we know about her problems," Belinda said. "It might make it a lot easier on her."

"I thought about that," Jessica said. "But you know Lila. She's too proud to accept our help. Not to mention stubborn. And besides, Melissa swore me to secrecy about this."

"Melissa couldn't actually have expected you to keep the secret," Janet said as she made out a list of committees on a notepad. "After all, it was your duty as a loyal Unicorn to tell us."

"What's that noise?" Kimberly asked suddenly. "It sounds like a freight train coming through your house—"

"Dog alert!" Steven yelled from the family room. "Look out, everybody!"

"Charlie! No!" Jessica screamed.

But it was too late. A soaking wet Charlie came bounding into the kitchen and headed straight for Jessica.

"The banner!" Mandy cried as Charlie pranced back and forth over the wet purple lettering, leaving purple footprints all over the sheet—and all over Jessica.

"Sorry," Steven said as he rushed over to grab Charlie. "I was trying to give him a bath, and he sort of escaped."

"The banner's ruined," Jessica moaned.

"Well, your 'W' was crooked, anyway," Ellen pointed out.

Charlie wagged his tail happily.

"Who does that disgusting mutt belong to, anyway?" Janet demanded.

"We're dog-sitting for a while," Jessica explained. "He belongs to a family at the shelter."

Janet rolled her eyes. "Another one of Elizabeth's do-gooder projects, right?" She made a face. "*Eau de wet dog*. My least favorite perfume."

Charlie twisted out of Steven's grip, bounded over, and placed his paws on Janet's lap. Then he planted a great big sloppy kiss on her face.

"Off, you smelly hound!" Janet screamed, shoving Charlie back onto the floor.

Charlie slid down to the floor and whimpered, as Janet gave him a shove with her foot.

"Don't you dare kick my dog!" Jessica cried, running over to protect him.

Charlie responded with a big, grateful kiss. Jessica groaned. "Can it, Charlie."

"I thought you hated dogs," Janet said as she brushed dog fur off her violet blouse.

"I don't hate dogs," Jessica said. "Dogs hate me." Charlie licked her again. "Most dogs, anyway," she added. "But somebody's got to watch out for Charlie while he's homeless. There are too many people like you around, Janet. *Real* dog-haters."

"Can you blame me?" Janet demanded. "Look at the mess he made."

"Come on, Charlie," Jessica said, leading him by the collar over to Steven. "Now you really do need a bath." She paused to examine the banner. "You know, I kind of like this paw print effect. Maybe Charlie should stick around for a while." She shot a glance at Janet. "We could even make him an honorary Unicorn."

"Over my dead—" Janet began, but she stopped in mid-sentence when Charlie began to growl at her.

"Don't tempt him, Janet," Jessica warned. "That's one thing about Charlie—he's a great judge of character."

Eleven

"There," Lila said proudly on Friday afternoon after school. "Not a bad unicorn, if I do say so myself." She held up the poster board she'd been drawing on. "Pin the tail on the unicorn—not a bad game idea, either."

"Nice work," Melissa said. She consulted her list. "Let's see. We've got all the decorations made."

"And a bunch of silly games to play," Lila added. "We're all set on entertainment, too," Melissa continued. "My dad's going to sing, of course. And you called Nora Mercandy's grandfather, right?"

Lila nodded as she put the finishing touches on her unicorn. "He said his magic act may be a little rusty, but he'd practice up before the party. And he promised not to tell Nora he was going to perform."

"Did you cancel the caterers and stuff?" Melissa asked as she removed a batch of cupcakes from the oven.

Lila nodded. "They're keeping the deposits, unfortunately. But I'm still going to save Daddy a bunch of money. I can't wait to tell him when he gets home tonight. He's going to be really impressed."

"So are the Unicorns," Melissa added.

Lila shook her head. "I'm not so sure about that. To tell you the truth, I'm beginning to think that the Unicorns may be starting to leave me out of things. The other day, Ellen said something about a meeting last Sunday."

"So?"

"So, there wasn't supposed to *be* a meeting last Sunday," Lila said quietly. "I think they may actually have had one without me. And there are other things, too."

Melissa sat down at the kitchen table and cupped her chin in her hands. "What kind of things?"

"They whisper around me. And they look at me strangely." Lila shook her head. "And to top it off, yesterday at the Unicorner Belinda said something about a party."

"Well, they were probably talking about the Fling," Melissa reassured her, although she wasn't entirely sure she believed it herself.

"Nope." Lila shook her head grimly. "Because as soon as Belinda said it, Jessica poked her in the ribs so hard she almost choked on her carrot stick."

Melissa was starting to get a sinking feeling that Lila's suspicions might be correct. "Here's what I don't get," she said slowly. "Why would the Unicorns be treating you any differently? You haven't told anyone about your dad, have you?"

"Just you," Lila said. "I think it's the little things the Unicorns have noticed. Like when Jess caught me shopping at a discount store. And my bringing a brown bag lunch to school. You have to admit, I haven't exactly been acting like myself lately."

Melissa shifted uncomfortably in her chair. "Well, just because you overheard Belinda say the word *party* doesn't prove anything."

"I hope you're right," Lila said glumly. "But I doubt it."

They sat there in silence, staring at the cupcakes.

"You definitely need some cheering up," Melissa said finally. She stood and reached for her purse. "Come on, I'm taking you shopping. My treat."

"Shopping?" Lila said. "Where to?"

"We're going to Party Time to buy some purple balloons!"

"That little store downtown?" Lila asked. "This is really nice of you, Melissa."

It's the least I can do, Melissa thought guiltily. She should never have trusted Jessica to keep a secret, that much was clear. It was obvious from the strange way the Unicorns were acting around Lila that they knew what was going on. She considered confronting Jessica and the Unicorns, but what would be the point? Lila was probably right to think they'd reject her if she was poor. After all, she knew them much better than Melissa did.

"You've turned out to be a great poverty adviser, you know that?" Lila said as they headed for the door.

But maybe not such a good friend, Melissa thought unhappily.

"Elizabeth and I thought it was really nice of you to invite the kids at the shelter to the Fling," Melissa said to Lila as the two girls crossed Main Street.

"I sort of felt it was my duty as a poor person," Lila said. "And besides, I ran out of stories to tell. It was the only way I could think to keep them occupied."

"Well, I'm sure the kids will have a great time. It'll be nice for them to get away from the day-care center for a little while."

"They'll probably be the only ones to show up," Lila joked lamely.

They were half a block from the party store when Lila suddenly grabbed Melissa's arm. "Look!" she whispered in a horrified voice. "Unicorns!"

Melissa followed Lila's gaze. There, coming out of the party store, were Jessica, Janet, Mandy, and Kimberly. They were all carrying large bags, and Jessica was hanging onto a bunch of purple helium balloons.

"I told you," Lila said softly. "They're having their own party."

Melissa felt a surge of anger. "I'm sorry, Lila," she said. "But don't worry. Other kids will come, even if the Unicorns don't. Your party's still going to be wonderful."

"How can it be, without my best friends there?" Lila asked miserably.

Melissa didn't answer. For the first time since she'd befriended Lila, she couldn't think of any good advice.

Lila buried her face in her hands. "It's over," she whispered. "I might as well face it. I'm not a Unicorn anymore."

"I never should have told Jessica the truth," Melissa muttered at the dinner table that night. "Never."

"You were just trying to help," Mr. McCormick said sympathetically as he passed a bowl of mashed potatoes to Andy.

"It's not your fault Jessica couldn't keep a secret," Andy added.

"But *I* couldn't keep it, either," Melissa said. "I feel lousy."

"Look at it this way, honey," Mr. McCormick said. "People were bound to find out about Lila sooner or later. You said she was planning on telling everyone at the party, anyway."

"But now there may not *be* anyone at the party," Melissa said. "No Unicorns at least. And they're the ones Lila wants there the most."

"Why don't you call them and find out?" Andy suggested.

"Go ahead," Mr. McCormick said. "Your dinner can wait."

"Thanks, Dad," Melissa said gratefully. She ran to the phone and dialed the Wakefields' number. "Is Jessica there?" she asked when Steven answered.

A moment later, she hung up the phone and returned to the kitchen table. "That was Jessica's brother," she said quietly. "He said she was over at Janet Howell's—working on stuff for their party."

"So Lila *was* right about them," Andy said.

"I've been telling Lila that it wouldn't matter

to her friends if she didn't have money anymore,"
Melissa exclaimed angrily. "But now it turns out
that it does matter!"

"The important thing is whether or not it matters to Lila," Mr. McCormick said gently.

"Try telling that to Lila tomorrow," Melissa
said sadly.

"My daughter, frosting a cupcake? I never
thought I'd see the day."

Lila looked up to see Mr. Fowler standing in
the kitchen doorway. "Daddy!" she exclaimed,
running over to give him a hug. "You're home!"

"I caught an early flight," Mr. Fowler said as
he took off his coat and set down his briefcase.
"These past couple weeks have been tough, and
I couldn't wait to get home. Besides, I knew you'd
need my help with the big party." He dipped his
finger into a bowl of purple frosting on the kitchen
counter. "Not bad," he said after he tasted it. "I'm
not so sure about the color, but it tastes good."

"And she made it herself," Mrs. Pervis said
as she bustled into the kitchen. She winked at Mr.
Fowler. "My theory is that she's been taken over
by an alien being."

"These aren't for the party, are they?" Mr.
Fowler asked, pointing to the plates of purple cupcakes on the counter.

"Yep," Lila said as she wiped her hands on
the apron she was wearing. "And there are plenty

more where those came from. Melissa McCormick and I have been baking all week."

Mr. Fowler sat down at the table. "But why, honey? You know that the caterers are going to take care of all this. Did you forget about the three-tiered cake?"

Lila sat down at the table and waited until Mrs. Pervis was safely out of earshot. "There's no need to be brave anymore, Daddy," she said gently. "We're in this together."

Mr. Fowler raised his eyebrows. "We are?"

"And it's nothing to be ashamed of, either. Melissa's been teaching me that." Lila smiled. "It's not so bad, once you get used to it. I even bought a blouse on sale this week, Daddy. Can you believe it?" She lowered her voice to a whisper. "It's half polyester, but it's actually kind of pretty."

"Lila, honey," Mr. Fowler said softly, reaching for her hand. "Is . . . uh . . . everything OK?"

Lila blinked. "I guess so," she said. "I'm holding up really well, under the circumstances."

"Maybe you could fill me in a little on exactly what the circumstances are."

"Daddy," Lila said. This was turning out to be harder than she'd thought. She was just going to have to be tough with her father. "I understand that you have to keep up appearances, but it's OK to admit that we're poor. I've adjusted already."

"Poor?" Mr. Fowler exclaimed.

"I know what this is," Lila said, pointing a finger at him. "Denial, I think it's called. I went through it, too. Then Melissa taught me how to bargain shop and clean the bathroom. I think that kind of broke through all my defenses."

"Lila!" Mr. Fowler cried, standing. "Enough, already. This is really an amusing little joke, but I just got home and I'm tired and—"

Lila shook her head sadly. Her poor father was trying so hard to pretend nothing had changed. "I don't mind being poor, really, Daddy." She paused. "Of course, I'm hoping I can keep my new CD player, but otherwise, I think I can get by."

Mr. Fowler crossed his arms over his chest and stared at her for a moment. "You're serious, aren't you?"

"Well, to tell the truth, I'd *rather* be rich, but—"

"So, you're really convinced that we're broke?"

Lila nodded.

"Where on earth would you get a notion like that?"

Lila got up and started pacing around the long kitchen table. Her father wasn't dealing with this nearly as well as *she* had. "First," she began, "there's the fact that we had to fire Randall."

"I fired Randall because he was stealing money that was supposed to be used to maintain our cars," Mr. Fowler replied.

"He *was*?" Lila cried, stopping in her tracks.

"Unfortunately, I've been so busy that it took me a while to notice the horrible condition he'd let them get into." Mr. Fowler shook his head. "Too bad, though. It may take a long time to find another chauffeur."

"I never *did* like Randall," Lila remarked distractedly. She was trying to remember exactly what Mrs. Pervis had said when she fired Randall. What was it? Something like *it has to do with the money*?

"You're a very wise girl," Mr. Fowler said. "Sometimes, anyway. So is that all your evidence that we're destitute?"

Lila resumed her pacing. "Well, there's the fact that my credit card was rejected at the mall."

"That was just a computer error, I'm sure. It happens sometimes."

"How about the fact that you said no to the hot-air balloon?"

"I just didn't have time to take care of all the arrangements for it. You know how busy I've been."

Lila patted her father on the shoulder. "You're being very noble, Daddy. But I heard you on the phone when you found out we were ruined."

Mr. Fowler's eyes clouded for a moment. "Oh!" he said suddenly. "You must have heard me talking about the Fairmont Software deal. Yes, I did lose a bundle on that one, but that same week another deal I put together made an even bigger bundle.'' He shrugged. ''That's business, honey. You win some, you lose some. But I'm still winning more than I lose, and we definitely are *not* broke. In fact, I suppose we've got more money than ever!''

Lila stopped and stared at him. ''You're telling me we're not ruined?''

''Not even close.''

''So I didn't need to cancel all the entertainment and caterers? Or make paper chains and pin the tail on the unicorn games? Or bake a zillion cupcakes?''

Mr. Fowler shook his head. ''No, honey. And I'm so sorry you were that worried. When I think how you wasted all that time trying to save money—''

Lila flopped back into a chair and rolled her eyes to the ceiling. All that work! All of it, a waste of time.

Then, suddenly, to her amazement, she felt a smile forming. ''It wasn't wasted time,'' she said thoughtfully. ''At least, not totally. I mean, I made a new friend. And it was a learning experience. I found out I could be as tough as any plain old regular person.''

''I'm very proud of you for being so strong,'' Mr. Fowler said. ''Not to mention for buying polyester.''

''I still prefer silk,'' Lila said quickly. ''In fact,

I think I'll donate that bargain blouse to Melissa's homeless shelter."

"You know, it's not too late for me to call some of the caterers and entertainment. You can still have the party you and the Unicorns were planning," Mr. Fowler said.

Lila's smile faded. "That's OK, Daddy," she said quietly. "There's no point in bothering. I found out one other thing while I thought I was poor."

"What's that?"

"Who my friends *really* are."

Twelve

◇

"Melissa, I've got something very important to tell you," Lila said on Saturday morning as the two girls hung a paper chain across the Fowlers' spacious backyard patio.

"I'm listening," Melissa said.

"Well, it's a little embarrassing," Lila said sheepishly. "You see—" she hesitated. "Uh, it turns out that I'm not as poor as I thought."

"You're not?" Melissa asked doubtfully.

"No." Lila shook her head. "In fact, I'm rich again. I mean still."

"You're kidding, right?"

"I guess I sort of overreacted," Lila confessed. "My dad says everything's fine."

Melissa laughed. "Well, that's great, Lila!" she cried. "I'm really glad for you."

"Are you sure?" Lila asked as she sat down on a lawn chair. "You don't hate me because I've got money again?"

Melissa shook her head. "It's not a crime to be rich."

"But I was afraid maybe that was the only reason we were friends," Lila admitted. "You know, because we were both poor. Just like the Unicorns only cared about me when I was rich."

"Lila, I like you either way," Melissa assured her. "I'm not sure why. I mean, you're a terrible snob, not to mention a lousy bargain shopper." She looked away. "But I'm not sure you're going to like me anymore when you hear what I have to confess."

"What?"

Melissa let out a long sigh. "I told Jessica about your being broke. I was just trying to help, and you were so worried about the Unicorns and all—"

"It's OK, Melissa," Lila interrupted with a wave of her hand. "It's just as well. I found out that all my friends really cared about was my money, anyway. I should be grateful to you."

"Still, I shouldn't have said anything."

"It doesn't matter now," Lila said. She was surprised at how simple it was for her to forgive Melissa. Lately, it had seemed easier than it used to be to tell what was really important in her life.

And she knew that Melissa's friendship mattered more than getting angry at her—especially since she had just been trying to help.

"I'm really glad you're my friend," Lila said sincerely. "I have the feeling I'm going to need one when this party flops."

"Think positively, Lila," Melissa scolded. "How can you look at all the work we've done and worry that this party's going to be a failure?"

Lila scanned her huge backyard. It did look wonderful, she had to admit. There were paper chains and purple balloons all over the trees and bushes. They'd set up a small stage for Mr. McCormick and Nora's grandfather to perform on. Tables were stacked with all kinds of homemade baked goods, most of them purple. On another table sat piles of the souvenir T-shirts Lila had ordered—the only part of the original Fling plans that she couldn't cancel.

"Look," Melissa said, pointing toward the street. "I see some people coming already."

"They're early," Lila said, glancing at her watch. She craned her neck to get a glimpse of the approaching car. "It's not the Unicorns, is it?" she asked hopefully.

Melissa shook her head. "I think it's some of the kids from the shelter."

Sure enough, an old battered green car made its way up the Fowlers' wide drive, and out piled Connie and the kids from the shelter.

Lila and Melissa ran to meet them.

"I'm so glad you all could come," Lila said. She was awfully relieved to have *some* guests, even if they weren't the Unicorns.

"Hey, we wouldn't have missed it for the world," Connie said. "It's all these kids have been talking about for days!"

A tall, lanky man got out of the car and smiled shyly. "That's my dad," David said. "He drove us over."

Just then, Mr. Fowler came out to join the group. "Dad," Lila said, "these are some friends of mine."

Mr. Fowler extended his hand to David's father. "Nice to have you," he said. He peered at the old green car Mr. Lowell had been driving. "Hey, *that* brings back memories. What year is that old jalopy, anyway?"

Mr. Lowell stood a little straighter. "It's sixteen years old," he said proudly. "But it runs like it just came off the showroom floor."

"I used to have one just like it when I was younger," Mr. Fowler said. "Best car I ever owned, to tell you the truth."

"They're a little hard to get parts for now," Mr. Lowell said. "But I manage."

"You're a mechanic, then?"

"He's a great mechanic," David said.

Mr. Fowler grinned. "I don't suppose I could talk you into taking a look at the big gas-guzzler

I've got in my garage?" he asked. "I'm getting an ugly sound out of the carburetor."

Mr. Lowell nodded thoughtfully as the two men headed up the driveway. "A backfire noise, or sort of a sucking sound?" he asked.

"Uh-oh," Lila said to Melissa. "That's the last we'll see of those two."

"Where's the Fink?" Sara asked, tugging on Lila's arm.

Lila grinned. "You mean the *Fling*, Sara."

"Where are the cupcakes?" Janie demanded.

"And the cookies?" David added.

Lila looked over at Melissa. "Come on," she said with a smile. "We've got some flinging to do!"

Soon dozens of other kids began to arrive and before long the yard was filled with people. Still, the Unicorns were nowhere to be seen. After a while Lila stopped looking for them. She knew it was hopeless. They were probably already at their own private party, having a wonderful time without her.

Melissa and Lila and Mrs. Pervis were kept busy attending to the guests. Mr. McCormick arrived and tuned up his guitar, and even Andy pitched in and helped organize the games.

"Great party, Lila," Ginny Lu Culpepper declared good-naturedly. "Folks back in Tennessee would never believe this spread!"

"I'm sure," Lila said. "Er, I mean, thanks." Ginny Lu wandered off to talk to Sophia Rizzo, and Lila looked around the backyard. Everywhere she looked she saw people having a good time. And kids she had barely said two words to in her life were coming up to tell her how much fun they were having.

"Cool party, Lila," Patrick Morris called out as he ran past her with a volleyball. Lila's father had helped her set up a net the night before, and some kids were starting up a friendly game. Lila grinned as she watched Amy Sutton and Jim Sturbridge arguing over who got to serve first.

"Lila?" Elizabeth called. "There's somebody over here I think you should meet."

Lila looked over to see a short plump man dressed in a business suit shaking hands with Elizabeth and Melissa. The man walked over and extended his hand to Lila. "Are you the hostess of this lovely event?"

"We both are," Lila said, nodding at Melissa.

"Well, I want to thank you so much for inviting me," the man said. "It's not every day I get to meet a herd of Unicorns! What are you, anyway? Some kind of service organization?"

For a moment, Lila considered explaining that she probably wasn't a Unicorn any longer. But it seemed like an awfully long story, and besides, she didn't even know this man. She wondered if he was a friend of her father's. "Well, sure," Lila said, "Unicorns try to do good deeds, I guess. Mostly we talk about boys, though."

The man laughed. "Well, I'm sorry I can't stay longer, but I'm afraid I've got a meeting to attend. I was lucky to be able to sneak away this long. Another party I was supposed to go to was canceled." He smiled. "Thanks for inviting me."

Lila cleared her throat. "I don't mean to be rude, but who *are* you, anyway?"

Melissa gave Lila a nudge from behind. "He's the mayor, Lila!" she whispered.

"The mayor? Here?" Lila gasped. "This is incredible!" she cried. "I feel like I should curtsy or something."

"Really, that won't be necessary," the mayor said. "But thank you, my dear. Now I really must be going."

"Take an extra cupcake," Lila urged. She ran to retrieve a T-shirt. "Here," she said, shoving the shirt into the mayor's hands. "Take a T-shirt, too."

The mayor took the shirt and cupcake and hurried off. Lila watched him leave and let out a big sigh. "If only the Unicorns had been here to see this," she said wistfully.

"See what?" asked a very familiar voice.

Lila blinked and spun around. "Jessica?" she cried, not sure she could believe her own eyes.

"And Operation Fling!" Jessica exclaimed, pointing toward the patio.

Lila watched in disbelief as all the Unicorns

filed out onto the back lawn. Each of them was carrying a huge tray. The trays held cakes, cookies, sandwiches, chips, and even a big bouquet of flowers made of purple tissue paper. Ellen brought up the rear, carrying a handful of purple helium balloons.

"We couldn't afford a *real* balloon," Ellen said apologetically. "But it's the thought that counts."

Lila stared at her friends, her mouth half-open, and slowly shook her head.

"Say something," Jessica urged.

"I don't get it," Lila said at last. "I thought you were having your own party. I thought you'd abandoned me!"

Jessica draped an arm around Lila's shoulder. "Lila," she said in a loud whisper. "Just because you're poor now, doesn't mean we're not still your friends."

"There is such a thing as Unicorn loyalty, you know," Tamara reminded her.

"That's why we launched Operation Fling," Janet added. "To show you that we'll stand by you, through thick and thin."

"After we eat all this food, we'll be more thick than thin," Belinda quipped as she set her tray of snacks on one of the tables.

"You mean you didn't care when you found out I was poor?" Lila asked.

"Of course we cared," Jessica joked. She

looked around at the Fowler estate and sighed. "We're going to miss all this, but we'll get over it. The point is, you're our friend, Lila. In a funny way, your becoming poor was a blessing in disguise. It helped us realize what being a Unicorn is really all about—friendship."

Lila felt her eyes well up with tears. "I feel terrible," she said. "How could I ever have doubted you guys?"

"I have a confession to make," Melissa admitted. "I had my doubts about you, too. To tell you the truth, I was beginning to think you Unicorns were nothing but superficial snobs."

"We *are* superficial snobs," Lila said with a laugh. "But that's just part of our charm." She lowered her voice. "I guess I should tell them, shouldn't I?" she asked Melissa.

"It's only fair," Melissa whispered back.

"Tell us what?" Jessica demanded.

Lila grinned. "I hate to disappoint you all, but there's been a little mistake."

"Mistake?" Kimberly echoed.

"My dad isn't broke, after all," Lila said.

A hush fell over the group.

"You made all that up?" Janet finally demanded.

"No, Janet, I didn't make it up. I really believed it. But it turns out everything's OK."

"You're telling us we didn't have to cook all this stupid food?" Jessica cried. "I made seventy-five bologna sandwiches this morning! Do you realize how much bologna that is?"

Melissa laughed. "Look on the bright side. We can donate all the extra food to the homeless shelter."

"I guess you're right," Jessica agreed, brightening. "And I *am* awfully relieved you're rich again, Lila." She paused. "Not that it matters how much money you have, or anything. But it's nice to have the old Lila back."

Lila grinned. "It's nice to be back."

Toward the end of the party all the guests gathered around the little makeshift stage to listen to Mr. McCormick sing. When the sun began to set, Lila looked up at the red and orange sky and smiled. "Nice sunset," she remarked contentedly.

"Nice party," Melissa responded.

Suddenly Lila gasped. As the sun slowly descended behind the house, something else was rising, and it was far too large and purple to be the moon.

"My balloon!" she cried. "My purple balloon!"

A hush fell over the crowd as the big balloon slowly rose over the house.

"Surprised?" Mr. Fowler asked with a smile.

"Astounded," Lila said. "You're a pretty cool dad, you know that?"

"I'd planned it all along, but I wanted to

surprise you," he said. "It's tethered out front. That's where they've been filling it."

"But what's that white thing hanging off the basket?" Lila asked, squinting to see in the twilight.

"The Unicorns gave it to me when they got here," he said.

" 'Welcome to Lila Fowler's Founding Fling,' " Lila read. She turned to the Unicorns. "Thanks, you guys. You're amazing."

As the balloon floated higher in the rosy sky, she peered a little closer. "You know," she said, shaking her head, "if I didn't know better, I'd swear those were dog footprints."

She looked over at Jessica and saw her exchange a grin with David.

"Was it Charlie?" he asked.

"He's really very artistic," Jessica replied.

"How is he?" David asked wistfully.

"He misses you tons," Jessica said. She looked over at Mr. Lowell, who had just joined the group. "Charlie asked me if maybe David could come by and visit next week."

"Could I?" David asked his father hopefully.

Mr. Lowell shook his head. "Son, I'm afraid that's out of the question," he said gently.

"But why?" David cried.

Mr. Lowell broke into a smile. "Because Charlie's going to be in his new house." He wrapped his arms around David. "*Our* house!"

"Our house?" David repeated in amazement.

"It seems I've got a new job," Mr. Lowell said.

"I've offered David's father a job as our new chauffeur," Mr. Fowler explained. "I've been looking all over for a good mechanic," he added, smiling at Lila. "Who'd ever have thought I'd find one at your Founding Flinging?"

"Fling," Lila corrected. She gave her father a hug and then turned her face to wipe away a tear.

"How come you're crying?" David asked. "Don't you get it? Charlie and my dad and me can have a house again!"

"You know how I like to tell stories," Lila said. She looked over at Melissa and smiled. "I guess I'm just a sucker for a happy ending."

Thirteen

$\Diamond$

"Wait, his bow is crooked," Jessica cried on Wednesday afternoon. She rushed up and knelt by Charlie's side. "I have to straighten this. Do you want him to look dumb?"

Elizabeth stood back and gave Charlie a critical look. "Jessica, do you really think a big purple bow is going to make him look *smart*?"

"He likes it," Jessica answered as she retied the bow to the back of Charlie's collar. He reached around, trying to pull the bow off, and when that failed he tilted his head and gave Elizabeth a pleading look.

"Actually, I think he's embarrassed by it," Melissa said with a laugh.

"Well, I don't care. I think he looks great," Jessica said.

"Whatever you say. Let's take him downstairs now. David and his dad will be here any minute."

"OK, OK," Jessica said. "Trust me. It's not as if I want to keep this flea-bag around any longer than I have to."

"Right," Elizabeth said, shaking her head. "I suppose that's why I caught you two sharing the same pillow this morning."

"If I don't let him share my pillow, he snores," Jessica explained. She leaned close to one of Charlie's ears. "Here's the deal, Mutt-breath. You're going back to your real owner now. David's dad has a new job—"

"Do you really think he's absorbing all this?" Melissa interrupted, grinning.

"Sure. He's very bright. For a slobbery, mangy old hound, I mean."

They heard the sound of the front door opening downstairs, and a moment later, Mrs. Wakefield's voice floated up. "Girls!" she called. "They're here!"

"Come on, Jess," Elizabeth said gently. "David will be waiting for Charlie."

"I suppose you're right," Jessica said, sighing heavily.

They were only halfway down the stairs when Charlie caught sight of David. He broke loose from Jessica's grip and went tearing down the stairs three at a time. David was nearly bowled over as he threw his arms around the dog.

"Girls, I really want to thank you for taking care of Charlie," Mr. Lowell said gratefully. "The worst thing to come out of this whole experience—losing my job and our home—was separating those two. And, thanks to you—and my son's sneakiness," he added, with a sidelong glance at David, "Charlie and David are finally back together."

"We were glad to help," Elizabeth said. "Charlie has been a perfect guest."

Jessica knelt down, and Charlie gave her his usual wet kiss. "He likes to sleep on a pillow, did you know that?"

"Did you say a pillow?" David asked.

"Well, he has this snoring problem—"

David grinned. "Whatever you say."

"Any time you need a dog-sitter," Jessica said hopefully. "I mean, if you ever have to go on vacation or anything and you need someone to take care of Charlie for a while—"

"You can come visit him whenever you want," David interjected.

Jessica cleared her throat. "Well, not that I'm into dogs or anything. But I might stop by now and then. Just to say hi."

"The only thing is, you can't put bows on him," David said sternly, pulling off the purple ribbon. "Bows," he muttered. "Pillows!" He opened the door and let Charlie run out onto the lawn. "Come on, boy," he said. "Let's go chase some cats or play catch or something. You've been around girls *way* too long."

"You know what?" Elizabeth said as they watched David and Charlie play. "I think maybe our volunteering did make a difference, after all."

"A very big difference," Mr. Lowell said softly.

"I didn't help, though," Jessica said in a guilty voice.

"Oh, yes you did," Elizabeth replied. "More than you realize." She patted her twin on the shoulder. "Just ask Charlie."

"I still can't believe the mayor was at our very own Fling," Jessica said as the Unicorns strolled through the mall the following week.

"I gave him a T-shirt, too," Lila said proudly.

"People are still talking about the Fling," Mandy said. "I think it will go down in history as the best party ever."

"And think of the money we saved," Lila mused as she led the group into Clothes Encounters. "My father donated it all to the shelter, did I tell you that?"

She headed straight to a table full of sweaters. "I'll take all of these," she said, waving her hand.

"All?" the clerk asked doubtfully.

"Here," Lila said, reaching into her wallet. "Charge it."

"Now, *that's* the old Lila," Ellen exclaimed. "Rich, extravagant, and very, very generous."

"This is so sweet of you, Lila!" Jessica added.

"Really, it's no big deal," Lila said with a grin.

The girls watched as the clerk loaded the sweaters into several bags and rang up the sale.

"See?" Lila said as she signed the credit card slip. "No problem, this time."

"Would you like help with all these bags?" the clerk asked.

"I'm sure my friends will give me a hand," Lila said confidently.

"It's the least we can do," Jessica added.

"It sure is nice to have such a wealthy friend," Ellen mused.

"Of course you like me rich or poor," Lila prompted.

"Of course!" the girls said quickly in unison.

"Thank you very much," the clerk said enthusiastically as the Unicorns grabbed the bags.

"I guess we should be saying thank you, too," Jessica said excitedly.

"You?" Lila said as the girls lugged the shopping bags out into the mall. "Why?"

"Well, because you're giving all your friends brand-new sweaters," Belinda said.

"Oh, these sweaters aren't for you," Lila said with a smile. "They're going to the shelter."

"The shelter!" Ellen exclaimed. She started to say something, then closed her mouth.

"Just help me carry them out to the car. David's dad should be waiting outside by now," Lila said.

"This is very generous of you, Lila," Jessica said sullenly.

"And noble," Janet added, frowning.

Lila grinned. "That's me, all right."

The girls continued walking, slowly carrying their heavy bags. A moment later Janet paused by a poster on one of the walls near the exits. "Look," she exclaimed. "Here's what you need, Ellen. Someone's opening a charm school, right here in Sweet Valley."

"Why would I need to go to charm school?" Ellen demanded.

Janet rolled her eyes. "To learn not to pick your teeth at parties. You should have seen yourself at the Fling."

"You're the one who ought to go, Janet," Ellen shot back. "I wonder if they have remedial classes for people who slurp through their straws."

"Run by Jacques and Monique Beaumont," Jessica read. "It says they're from Switzerland." She smiled. "I'd love to go to charm school! They teach you vital things, like how to walk with a book on your head like a fashion model."

"And proper mascara application," Tamara added.

"We already *know* that," Lila reminded her.

"Well, I'm definitely going to sign up," Jessica vowed. "Not that I need any training in charm!"

Will the Unicorns make the grade at charm school? Find out in Sweet Valley Twins no: 64, **THE CHARM SCHOOL MYSTERY.**